TAKE THE HIGH ROAD

TAKE THE HIGH ROAD

Danger in the Glen
by
Michael Elder

Scottish Television

This book is published by

SCOTTISH TELEVISION
Cowcaddens
Glasgow G2 3PR

in conjunction with

MAINSTREAM PUBLISHING
25a South West Thistle Street Lane
Edinburgh EH2 1EW

ISBN 0 906391 56 3

First edition 1984
Reprinted 1985

Typeset by Spectrum Printing Company, Edinburgh.
Printed in Great Britain by Collins, Glasgow.

Executive Producer ROBERT LOVE
Producer   BRIAN MAHONEY
Script Writers   PETER MAY
                     TOM WRIGHT
                     BILL CRAIG
                     WILLIAM ANDREW
                     MICHAEL ELDER
Series Devised by   DON HOUGHTON

Prologue

Dougal lay with his nose in a patch of dead heather and waited. The day was of a startling clarity. Ben Darroch and its attendant peaks stood out sharply against the steel blue of the sky. Yet to the west there was a hint of mistiness, confirming the weather report he had heard—that there was a thaw on the way.

Achilles must come soon.

Dougal clutched the rifle in his right hand and raised his head slightly to peer through the crevice between two stones at the view down into the narrow gully ahead of him. For days now he had laid out a trail of beech nuts, leading ever closer to this natural hide, tempting Achilles nearer to him. So far he had been lucky. Winds could be fickle at this height but there had been very little in the cold stillness of the early March days and what there was had always blown towards him from the gully. Now there was talk of milder weather which would draw Achilles higher into the hills and therefore into less acessible parts. Furthermore a change in the weather would probably mean a change in the wind direction, and if it swung behind Dougal now all his preparations would have been in vain.

The deer farm on the lower slopes of Ardvain was complete and stocked with hinds from the hills. Throughout the winter Dougal and the other crofters had worked at bringing them in from the higher fastnesses of the Glendarroch estate and now they could do it with practised ease. Maybe later, when the farm began to show some financial return for their efforts, they would be able to buy in stock from other deer farms or exchange animals to prevent too much inbreeding and keep the stock strong. But that was some distance away yet. Most of these hinds were pregnant when they were brought in and by June there would be a fair crop of calves but, looking to the future, Dougal knew that the most important addition to the herd he was trying to establish was a first-class stag.

And Achilles was undoubtedly that stag.

He had first spotted Achilles through his telescope when he was searching for hinds one day just before Christmas. He had just immobilised one in Corrie Vrannichan on the west face of the Ben when movement higher up on the slope of the mountain caught his attention. And there he was, on the crest of the ridge, a magnificent fourteen pointer, his proud head turned disdainfully in Dougal's direction as though he were contemptuously watching the pigmy aspirations of mortal men below. And Dougal had marked him for his first stag. The name had crossed his mind at that time. Vaguely he was aware that Achilles was some kind of ancient Greek hero, a superman among men. He didn't know much more about him except that people talked about him sulking in his tent, whatever that meant, but the name seemed appropriate for this magnificent king among beasts. Mature and strong with several years of top class breeding in him, Achilles would strengthen the herd in the deer farm in the early days.

Suddenly his thoughts came back to the present, for there was movement behind the rocks beyond the little gully, and then the dull red of the stag's body seemed to detach itself from the surrounding scree and the majestic head of antlers moved forward.

Dougal clutched the rifle, watching, waiting.

Achilles came forward, lowering his head to pick up some of the beech nuts Dougal had strewn on the rough ground, then raising it again to gaze in a lordly manner round the immediate area of his kingdom. There was nothing scared in that glance. It was imperious, noble. But Dougal knew that one wrong move could send Achilles with what seemed the speed of light up the slope into the inaccessible heights of Ben Darroch.

Achilles was seventy-five yards away. Too far for a certain shot, even in this perfect light. But the trail of beech nuts led Achilles inexorably towards Dougal. Subconsciously Dougal assessed the wind direction. It was still blowing very gently into his face. Achilles would not catch his scent.

The .22 rifle was ready. Very gently now he drew it into his right shoulder, feeling the familiar stock nestling there, his cheek along the smooth, sleek wood.

Achilles came forward, stepping on delicate feet over the scree and stones. He was totally exposed now, and

Dougal felt some compunction at what he was about to do. It suddenly seemed wrong. But he fought the feeling down, telling himself not to get sentimental.

Fifty yards.

Achilles was clear in the sights.

He had never been so close before and once again he smiled in admiration. Even for March he was in beautiful condition. By now the effects of the winter and the difficulty of finding food should have told in Achilles's appearance but, perhaps because of the beech nuts with which Dougal had been luring him over the last week or so, he showed no signs of malnutrition.

Achilles cropped another few beech nuts and then raised his head. Forty yards, and something had alerted him. Some instinct had warned him that all was not as it should be. Dougal was fairly sure Achilles could not see him, but the regal head was turned in his direction and the soft but arrogant eyes seemed to be staring straight at him.

This was the moment.

Dougal's finger tensed on the trigger.

At that moment instinct took Achilles over completely. If there is something you don't understand, get away from it, instinct shrieked. And with what might have been a disdainful toss of his head, shaking those beautiful four-teen point antlers, Achilles turned and prepared to take off for the higher ground. But as he turned for a split second he exposed his haunch and Dougal fired.

The dart, impelled by the blank cartridge in the .22, hit true. Dougal knew exactly what was happening. The rubber washer round the hole in the needle was forced backwards by the impact with the stag's hide and the pressure pumped into the tube of the dart sent the two millilitres of Immobilon into Achilles's system. The job was done.

Though you wouldn't think so from Achilles's reaction. The report from the rifle brought reality to instinct and in an instant those long, strong legs were taking the stag across the face of the Ben at an enormous rate.

Dougal sighed and stood up, stretching cramped limbs, and reached for the thermos of tea in his pack. Already it seemed not so cold and the mistiness in the west was turning into a lowering layer of cloud. Rain was coming and Achilles would probably head high.

There was relief in his sigh, too. He was glad to be rid of the Immobilon in the dart. Dangerous stuff. Prick yourself on the needle when you were loading the dart and you'd be dead in three minutes unless you could get a dose of the antidote, Revivon, into you in that time. But it worked less violently on the deer for whom it was designed. Achilles might travel a couple of miles, but the drug was already active in him and eventually he would keel over and simply fall asleep.

Dougal turned and headed down the slope to the point where he had left the Argocat. He would follow Achilles in that, its eight wheels taking it over the worst of terrains, until he caught up with the sleeping stag. He would load him into the back of the Argocat and take him gently down to the farm where he would administer the Revivon, and Achilles would have a new home. A confined home, perhaps, though there wasn't all that much confinement in the one hundred and fifty acres of the deer farm, and he would have an assured supply of food and hinds for the rutting season. His life would be different but, Dougal was sure, pleasanter.

And the future of the deer farm would be assured with the addition of its first first-class stag.

Chapter One

1

It was one of those mornings when everything seemed to have gone wrong. To begin with George Carradine wasn't in his office and Elizabeth urgently wanted to consult him. Some of the tenants were making noises as usual about their leases, and it would be best if she could placate them and give them an answer today. And George was away fishing, if you please. On a Friday. Really, did lawyers ever do any work at all?

Then there was Fiona. What was she to do with her? Ever since that disastrous affair with Geddes of the Home Farm and that—accident?—when Fiona had fallen from her horse, she had been totally unapproachable, had erected a barrier against the world so that no more pain could get in. It was natural, Elizabeth supposed, remembering her own unhappy parting from Peter, but the girl should really have been snapping out of it by now.

And the third thing was that Lorna was late. If Elizabeth had stopped to think rationally she might have wondered why Lorna was late and perhaps have worried that something might have happened to her. Lorna was never late. But such was Elizabeth's state of mind today that she could not think in those terms. It was simply another pinprick to add to the many which she felt were being unfairly thrust into her at the moment.

She needed Lorna here. There was a mound of work to get through this morning, and she looked with dismay at the piles of papers to be dealt with, official forms to be filled in, official letters to be answered, brochures to be read, statements from the bank to be frightened by, which lay there in a seemingly bewildering mess and felt once more, as she had felt so often recently, that everything was falling in on top of her. It was all very well saying that she could do without a factor. The estate was in such a condition that it couldn't afford a factor, but it was really becoming too much for her, and when her secretary was late and her lawyer had gone fishing and her daughter was unwilling or unable to help in the way she had hoped and expected, she felt she had good ground for complaint.

She got up from her desk in the office and went through to the reception room. Lorna was still not there. The cover was still on her typewriter and there was no coat hanging on the stand. Elizabeth quelled her impatience with an effort and for the first time began to wonder if something had happened. It wasn't like Lorna to be late. She organised her life very efficiently and if she had intended to be late she would have said so last night, sought permission or offered an explanation . . . Could she ring someone in the village and ask them to go and see if all was well at Lorna's cottage? Hardly. Leave it for another half hour or so. If by that time she hadn't shown up Elizabeth would know that something serious had indeed happened. Even as she made the decision she heard the sound of the front door open and close and feet tapping rapidly along the stone floor of the hall towards the door. Elizabeth's concern disappeared and impatience returned. She looked at her watch. It was a quarter past nine.

The door opened and Lorna, looking slightly windswept, came in.

"Where have you been?" Elizabeth demanded sharply. "I particularly wanted to get started early this morning. There are the vaccination returns to be got out—"

"I'm sorry, Mrs Cunningham," Lorna broke in a little breathlessly. "I went round by Laird's Point . . ."

Laird's Point. Was this to be the fourth thing to go wrong this morning? Laird's Point had been a running sore in Glendarroch for almost as long as Elizabeth could remember. How it ever came to be a piece of Crown land in the middle of the estate she was not very sure, though doubtless George Carradine would be able to explain it to her if she gave him half a chance. And if he wasn't fishing. It had been taken over by the Ministry of Defence and they had built something there. Rumour was rife in the village as to what it actually was. She remembered the furore created when Maggie Ferguson had been arrested for leading a protest outside the gates against—what was it?—a germ factory or something equally absurd. The Ministry of course never said a word and it had all died down since whatever it was they built there had been finished. There was nothing to see. Most of the structural work was underground and there was hardly ever anyone to be seen manning the place, giving rise to the view that it was entirely automatic and that sooner or later the village would be overrun by a posse of robots.

"What's happening at Laird's Point?" she asked, forgetting her earlier anger at Lorna's tardiness.

"I don't know. I was on my way here and I suddenly noticed a lorry heading down the track towards the gate. A big, heavy lorry with a covered load. So I followed it."

"And?"

"There are men working inside the perimeter wire, Mrs Cunningham."

"Did you ask what they were doing?"

"No, I didn't. They didn't see me. I was late already, so I just turned and came back. But I thought you ought to know."

"You're quite right, Lorna. Thank you . . . Laird's Point again. I thought we had finished with that."

She perched on Lorna's desk, worrying about this new problem while Lorna hastily took off her coat and began to prepare for the day's work.

"These men. Were they servicemen?"

"I don't think so. They didn't look like it, and they certainly weren't wearing any kind of uniform."

"How many?"

"I only saw one or two. Besides the driver of the lorry."

"You didn't see what was in the lorry?"

"No. It was closed and the flap was done up at the back."

One of the other theories about what was happening at Laird's Point was some kind of distant early warning system, and there had been disappointment when huge aerials hadn't sprouted from the ground like metallic mushrooms. Maybe this was the start of the metallic mushrooms now. It was so difficult to know what on earth the Ministry of Defence might be planning. It was more than possible that the Ministry itself didn't know, either. But what happened at Laird's Point affected the estate. She had dreaded the thought of aerials springing into the sky in the midst of some of the most glorious scenery in Scotland and had felt a sense of enormous relief as time had passed and no such things had appeared. Was that relief to prove premature now? It wasn't just the fact that an area of natural beauty would be spoilt, she told herself realistically. It would also spoil the view from the south-facing windows of Glendarroch House, for any such structure would be easily visible from there. And she didn't want that to happen. What could she do?

Damn George Carradine and his fishing expedition. He would have advised her.

But in his absence she could take some action herself. If there were men working there she could go and ask them what they were doing. In all likelihood they wouldn't know, but at least she would have done something towards finding out. And she would have established her presence, even if not her authority.

"I think I'll go down and see what's happening, Lorna," she said. "I'll only be about half an hour."

"Right, Mrs Cunningham. I'll get these vaccination returns done while you're away."

"Thank you," said Elizabeth and she went out into the hall.

She hadn't got a coat down here because she had not intended to leave the house this morning, so she climbed the stairs to the flat to get one. It was the middle of March and still very cold.

Fiona was in the sitting room, sprawled in a chair, a magazine open on her lap, but it didn't look as if she had been reading it. Or if she had she was showing an inordinate interest in a lawnmower which was guaranteed to cut grass without, so far as she could see, any effort on the part of its owner. Archie would like that, but it was hardly Fiona's scene. Fiona looked up as she came in and then, without expression or acknowledgement, looked down again.

Elizabeth felt herself unsure in the presence of her daughter these days. It was a disconcerting and un-comfortable feeling, one which she did not enjoy. She wished she could break through to her, elicit some response from her, but there was nothing.

"I'm going down to Laird's Point," she said. "Like to come?"

For a moment Fiona didn't reply and then she laid the

magazine aside as though she regretted not being able to read more about the lawnmower.

"All right," she said.

But there was no enthusiasm in her voice. Neither was there resentment nor interest, hardly even boredom. There was just—nothing. But Elizabeth, illogically, had the feeling that she might have scored some kind of minor victory in persuading Fiona actually to do something, however pointless. It was as though contact might have been established again.

"Better get a coat. It's cold out there," she said brightly, trying to show approval of Fiona's action without actually saying so because that might have caused her to change her mind and refuse to come.

Ten minutes later they were walking down the path to the wall at the foot of the kitchen garden. It looked barren just now. It was time Archie took it in hand, and she made a mental note to remind him of it when she got back to the house. There was a gate in the boundary wall which led out into fields and from there a footpath led down in turn to the loch side.

It was a beautiful day, cold and crisp and yet with the first hint of a possibility of spring in the air. The water of the loch was glassy calm, and from here it was impossible to tell where the opposite shore ended and reflection began. Around them the mountains reared grey and solid, the purple of the autumn heather long gone, the green of the spring growth not yet apparent, the cracks and scars on their eastern faces highlighted by the low early-morning sun. Elizabeth took a deep breath and felt the joy of the place wash through her as it had done all her life. This was hers and this was where she belonged. She glanced at Fiona's white, set face. There was a time when she too would have relished a morning like this to some extent, but that had been long ago. She wondered if Fiona ever would again.

It was important that she should. Fiona was the last of the Peddies, the end of a line which stretched back into the unknowable past. A Peddie had fallen with James IV at Flodden. There had been a Peddie with Bruce at Bannockburn. There had been heroic Peddies and cowardly Peddies, brilliant Peddies and unutterably stupid

Peddies, but the line had gone on till now it looked as if it might all come to an end. Not with a bang but a whimper. Elizabeth had no brothers. Fiona had no brothers. Already the name was dead, but the family home was still in the direct line.

Yes, Fiona must be made to care again . . .

They came down to the loch side and walked along the shingle at its edge, little waves rolling gently in to the shore beside them. There must be a breeze out in the middle to cause these, thought Elizabeth.

Ahead of them the promontory of Laird's Point jutted into the loch. It was a bare area which had once been covered with scrubby bushes and rowan trees, but the Ministry had rooted them out for whatever mysteries they had performed, and the area was cordoned off with a high and very effective wire fence leading right down into the water at either side of the promontory so that, although access might have been affected by someone desperate enough to get in, the intention to keep people out could not have been plainer. The track from the main road led down to the shore and entered the fenced-off area by a padlocked gate. This was closed, the padlock in place, and there was no sign of the lorry which Lorna claimed to have seen.

Within the fenced-off area there were one or two small structures which looked like concrete blockhouses, but there was little else to see, and Elizabeth understood that whatever was there was mainly underground. This air of mystery had of course excited the most intense speculation, speculation which had grown wilder as it became less satisfied. Elizabeth had a feeling that it was not going to be satisfied now.

There was also, she saw, what looked like some kind of fresh machinery lying under plastic sheeting near one of these blockhouses, another of which was evidently being used at the moment as some kind of an office, for she could see that the door was open, revealing three men standing just inside engaged in what looked like a relaxed chat. In a way it was quite a relief to find that there were actually human beings inside the Laird's Point enclosure.

The men paid no attention to them, though Elizabeth was sure that she and Fiona had been seen.

She stood at the gate for a moment, watching them with mounting irritation. One of the men came out of the office and turned away towards a further blockhouse. His gaze swept her, offered her no recognition or acknowledgement and he went on. The remaining two followed him and one turned to lock the door while the other waited.

"Good morning," called Elizabeth coldly.

They were youngish men, she saw when they turned to face her. Possibly brothers, for there seemed to be a family resemblance in their faces, though not so much in their builds. The one she took to be the older was about six feet tall and broad shouldered. His hair was dark and he had a growth of beard which half hid a face drawn with lines of discontent. The other was slighter in build and not so tall. He too was dark, but he had taken the trouble to shave if not that day at least the day before, and his face, though similar in shape to the other's, had an altogether more gentle look about it. It was this one who responded.

" 'Morning," he said.

"Can I have a word with you?" Elizabeth asked.

The older one stuck his hands in the pockets of his denims and came forward with what seemed to be a mixture of truculence and contempt.

"I canna stoap ye," he said.

Glasgow from their speech, thought Elizabeth. Funny. Somehow she had thought if they were from the Ministry of Defence they would have had English accents, though she acknowledged that there was no logic in that thinking at all.

"What are you doing here?" she asked.

The older man on the other side of the gate stopped and stared at her. The stare confirmed her earlier impression. There was truculence and contempt in it.

"What's it to you?" he asked.

Elizabeth bridled at his tone.

"This is my land," she said. "What happens next door to it concerns me."

"Oh. It's your land, is it?" said the older one, and Elizabeth immediately place the type. He was one of those who thought that all people who owned land were immensely rich, living like some Victorian factory owner off the sweated labour of the poor who lived on their land.

It was a way of thinking which was as prevalent as it was inaccurate.

"Yes, it is," she said.

"Well, is that no interesting? Ye hear that, Stevie? We're talking to the laird. Give your forelock a bit tug, man."

"Shut up, Joe," said the younger one, evidently in some embarrassment.

"Don't you think I've a right to know what my next door neighbour's doing on his property?" asked Elizabeth, trying to be as reasonable as possible.

"Ah, well, if your next door neighbour's doing things with his property, ye'd best ask your next door neighbour himself. No me. And no Stevie, neither. We just do the work."

"I see. Well, I know the next door neighbour is the Minister of Defence, but I don't think I can go and ask him," said Elizabeth.

"Oh. Is he no dining with ye tonight?"

Elizabeth forced herself to remain calm. The man was deliberately trying to anger her and she was determined that she would not let him see how well he was succeeding. She glanced at Fiona and in a strange way got some comfort from the unconcerned face. Fiona was staring at the younger man with no sign of interest, and Elizabeth returned to the other, her temper under control again.

"No," she said. "And I take it you don't get your orders directly from him?"

The man grinned without humour and without further response.

"So who do you take your orders from?" she asked.

"Now, can ye think of wan good reason why I should tell ye?"

"Yes. It would save a bit of time. But I shall find out in the end."

He looked as if he was preparing for another insulting remark when the younger one interrupted hastily.

"Henderson and Speirs," he said.

"Shut your mouth, Stevie," said the one called Joe. "Ye don't need to tell the likes of her nothing."

"Thank you," said Elizabeth to Stevie. "Henderson and Speirs, the contractors in Auchtarne?"

"Got it in wan, lady, got it in wan," said Joe in mock admiration.

"Thank you," said Elizabeth. "I will get in touch with them since you don't seem inclined to tell me what you're doing yourselves."

"We don't ken, missus," said the younger one. "We just get our orders and do what we're tellt. That's all there is to it, and—"

"Shut up, Stevie," said Joe. "Leave her to her land and her big hoose and all her la-di-da friends—"

"I thank you for your civility," said Elizabeth to Stevie. "But not yours," she added, finding herself trembling with anger in spite of herself. "Come along, Fiona."

"Oh, Fiona, is it?" said Joe. "Good morning, my lady. Good morning, Miss Fiona."

Elizabeth turned away furiously and had gone half a dozen paces when she realised that Fiona was not with her. She turned and found that she was still at the gate, staring at the two men.

"Fiona," she said sharply.

And Fiona turned and came towards her obediently but, Elizabeth thought, evidently with some reluctance. In the midst of her burning anger at the way the older man had treated her she felt a sense of interest—Fiona seemed to have responded somehow to something, for the first time since the Geddes affair.

But that thought didn't last. She was too concerned with her encounter with the men at Laird's Point. Too angry. Whatever they were doing she would do her best to stop it.

2

There seemed to have been a great deal of activity around the house this morning. People going out early and coming in late. It had all been slightly exhausting and Archie headed for the kettle in the reception room with a sense of relief. A quick cup of tea before he began to think about what he should do this morning would do wonders for the system.

He had almost made it when the front door slammed and

Mrs Cunningham strode in with Fiona following silently. More like her mother's shadow than ever, he thought.

"Archie," she said sharply, so sharply that he let go of the tea pot which he had just picked up as though it were red hot.

"Aye, Mrs Cunningham, good morning," he said, "I was just going to have a look at that blocked drain—"

"Archie, what's happening at Laird's Point?"

Archie felt relieved. He had wondered what little oversight of his Mrs Cunningham's hawk-like eyes had lighted on now. He knew that tone of voice only too well.

"I'm sure I don't know, Mrs Cunningham," he said.

Lorna looked up from her typewriter.

"Did you see them, Mrs Cunningham?" she asked.

"I did, Lorna. I most certainly did. They were insufferably rude. Told me to get in touch with Henderson and Speirs in Auchtarne if I wanted to know what they were up to."

"Henderson and Speirs?" said Archie. He shook his head gloomily. "That place hasna been the same since old Bob Henderson died. The man Speirs is a—a go-getter." It was the best word he could use considering the company though one or two more appropriate ones sprang to mind. "Wouldna trust him, Mrs Cunningham."

"I'm going to speak to him anyway," she said.

"Do you want me to get him for you, Mrs Cunningham?" asked Lorna.

"Yes, please, Lorna."

Lorna pulled out the telephone directory and began to search for the number.

"Do you know anything about what's going on there, Archie?" Mrs Cunningham asked.

"No, Mrs Cunningham. I know they've been working at the place for a wee while now. Maybe a week."

"I should have been told."

"Sorry, Mrs Cunningham. I thought you knew."

"And you've no idea what they're doing?"

Archie shook his head. It was a funny thing. Everyone in Glendarroch knew that there were men working at Laird's Point—except the lady laird herself, apparently—but no one knew what they were doing and efforts to find out had so far proved useless. He reported all this to Mrs

Cunningham as she waited impatiently for the telephone call to be put through. It didn't really amount to very much and he could see that she wasn't satisfied.

"The men come over from Auchtarne each day on the ferry. Jimmy Blair told me about them. They keep themselves to themselves though."

"Well, I shall certainly have a word to say to Mr Speirs about their manners. A couple of complete boors. Oh. And Archie—"

Archie braced himself.

"Yes, Mrs Cunningham?"

"That kitchen garden needs attention. See to it, will you? Thank you, Lorna."

She took the receiver which Lorna held out to her and Archie looked longingly at the kettle on the filing cabinet. If only he'd started making his tea ten minutes earlier he might have been able to slip away with a cup now.

"Archie."

Archie tried not to show surprise.

"Yes, Miss Fiona?" he said.

"They're not all bad, are they?" Fiona asked.

"Who?"

"The men at Laird's Point."

"I don't know, Fiona. I've never spoken to any of them."

"One of them was pretty rude. But not the other one."

She stared at Archie for a moment and then without another word turned and left the room. Archie stared after her. It was the first time she had spoken to him voluntarily since her mother had brought her back from the home.

3

Joe MacMorran watched the two women walk away from the gate, and spat on the ground.

"Stuck up bitch," he said.

"Och, I don't know," said Stevie.

"See the way she looked at us? And the way she spoke? As if we was the scum of the earth. That's the way these folk think, Stevie."

"I didn't see it like that, Joe."

Joe looked at his younger brother pityingly. God knows,

he'd tried to teach Stevie the facts of life, but the lad seemed curiously slow to learn. And Stevie had had the same upbringing as himself. He'd seen what life was like in Easterhouse. He'd known the same drunken, brutal father and the same whining, helpless mother. He'd seen the furniture taken away when there was no money to pay the rent. It was odd that Stevie couldn't see the basic injustices the same as he could.

But Stevie was soft, that was all there was to it. A good lad, but soft. Maybe he'd toughen up in time. After all, he was only twenty. Joe was twenty-five and vastly more experienced. Been inside too, he thought with some pride, remembering the car he'd nicked one Sunday night in the posh end of Glasgow. Standing outside one of those great rich houses with trees in the garden in a quiet street in the angle of Byres Road and Great Western Road. Owned by someone who'd never miss the bloody car and could buy a couple more next day if he wanted to. But they'd got him, and there had been other things to take into account, so it meant a few months' rest inside where he'd met some interesting folk. Stevie'd never had that chance yet, though no doubt the time would come, And no bad thing. That had been Joe's baptism of fire. That had been what made a man of him. Taught him the way to go about things properly, let him meet the right people.

But *that,* he thought, as he watched the two back views disappearing along the loch side, was what made for the injustice. Owned all this land, did she, that stuck-up bitch and the peely-wally lassie beside her who looked as if she was bored out of her mind getting her photograph in the *Tatler* yet again.

"That's what she thinks we are, Stevie, you mark my words. The scum of the earth, that's what we are to her. But don't you believe it, my lad. We're not the scum of the earth. It's her and her kind that's the scum of the earth."

"Aye, that'll be right, Joe," said Stevie, but it didn't sound as if he meant it.

"And I'll tell you this, she's no going to get away with it."

"What are you thinking aboot, Joe?"

Funny the way that reserved note came into Stevie's voice then. As though he disapproved of doing anything about standing up for your rights. As though he was content to let folk like those two trample all over them any time of the day or night they chose to do it. Well, it would change. Come the revolution. They laughed at that idea, but Joe knew that a revolution was long overdue. And if he could find a way of taking a step towards starting it he'd do it like a shot. You had to hit these people. Hit them hard. And where it hurt. In their pockets. Their property.

Well, perhaps something could be done about that, because just yesterday Joe had seen somebody who might give him a lead . . .

"I'm just thinking there's maybe a way I can find out how to do it," he said.

4

Dougal located the herd near the top of the lower hill. They hadn't yet moved down into the really low ground, but the fact that they'd come off the heights was a sign that warmer weather was gradually creeping in. He stopped the Argocat and rattled the bag of beech nuts, and one or two of the hinds, recognising the noise and understanding what it meant, moved towards him.

It was strange how tame the deer became. It only took a week or two for them to realise that food in the farm was far more plentiful than it was outside where they had to forage for themselves, and that the winter feed which they normally found so scarce was actually supplied from this mechanical vehicle with the eight wheels by a strange two-legged individual who seemed to wear it like a hide.

He threw some beech nuts towards them and they stooped daintily to recover them from the ground. Dougal examined them critically from the Argocat. There was a tell-tale swell in their bellies now which showed that they were in calf, and as far as he could tell the numbers in the farm would be swollen by five or six dozen calves by the end of June. It had been a hard winter's work but now he could sit back for a little and enjoy his success.

And there was the hero himself, standing further up the hill. Achilles, with his magnificent fourteen points which he would be shedding in a month or so from now. Dougal drove the Argocat towards him. The noise didn't worry Achilles at all. Dougal stopped a few yards from him and the stag stood motionless, watching him. It was probably Dougal's imagination but that old imperious look seemed to have gone now, and the stag looked at him with a friendlier eye. So he should. He was feeding well, thanks to Dougal, much better than he would have done in the open, and he really was in prime condition. When the rut started in September he would sire many good calves.

Achilles deigned to move towards the Argocat. Dougal rustled the bag of beech nuts and pulled some out. But this time instead of flinging them on the ground in front of Achilles he held a couple of them out in his hand. Achilles hesitated as though for the first time in his life he felt unsure. He took a delicate step forward, nostrils twitching as he picked up the longed-for scent of the beech nuts. Then he stepped forward again, stretched out his neck and quickly took one of them. For a split second Dougal sensed the soft mouth against his hand and he felt a thrill of pleasure at the physical contact between himself and this creature of the wild who had never been touched by a human before .

But he forced the pleasure away. He must not become emotionally involved with these animals. If he did, when the time came he would find it impossible to do what would have to be done, and that was shoot Achilles, not this time with an anaesthetising dart but with a proper bullet to bring to an end a life which would by then have started to go rapidly downhill as old age and possible disease began to take their toll.

There was, thought Dougal, enormous pleasure to be had from running a deer farm, but like most things in life, the pleasure was always mixed with something of pain.

5

George Carradine's office looked like something out of Dickens, Elizabeth thought as she looked round the dark old shelves crowded with dusty volumes, the huge desk piled with important-looking papers bound with pink tape, and the heavy curtains at the windows which looked out over the bustling Auchtarne High Street. Did anyone ever select one of those volumes, she wondered, blow the dust off it and actually read what was printed inside? Did anyone ever slip one of those pink tapes off a pile of documents and study the document itself? Were those curtains ever drawn across the windows on a cold winter's night to keep the darkness out? She didn't know. And it was too fanciful to ask George who probably wouldn't understand what she was driving at. He himself seemed alien here. Not that he was more up to date. Just out of place. He gave the impression of being some imperturbable Buddha as he sat quietly on the other side of the desk and peered at her through his glasses.

She had rung first thing that Monday morning for an appointment as soon as possible and had then driven over to see him. She knew he would have come to her, but she wanted to make the journey, tell him she had needed his advice on Friday when he hadn't been here and had now put herself out to come to Auchtarne. Maybe that would stir his conscience. When it came to the bit, she didn't tell him about Friday, even though she felt that had he been contactable then she might have avoided the unpleasant encounter with those two young men at Laird's Point. But common sense told her she couldn't blame him. He worked hard, she knew, and it was unfortunate that one of the days when he had decided to take a break should coincide with her urgent need of his advice.

And now as she listened to him she realised that he had already been busy on her behalf.

"I had much the same trouble with Speirs as you seem to have had," he said.

"He was uncooperative?"

"Tried to pull the Official Secrets Act on me. I laughed at him."

"Was that wise, George?"

"I don't know. But I enjoyed it. I don't like him as a person. Between you and me I think he sails pretty close to the wind legally sometimes."

"So you got nowhere either?"

"I didn't say that. He wasn't particularly forthcoming. At first. Then I threatened him, I'm afraid."

"Threatened him?"

"Yes. Said I would take the matter to a higher authority at the Defence Ministry in London unless I could get some kind of a satisfactory answer from him."

"And did you?" she asked.

He grimaced slightly.

"Not altogether, but probably as much as we shall ever get without resort to a great deal of effort which might prove unproductive in the end. Speirs admitted that they have received a contract to dismantle the site."

"Dismantle it?"

"Yes."

"But they only built it a couple of years ago."

"Yes."

"At enormous trouble and cost."

"Yes."

"And so far as we know it's never been used."

"Not so far as we know."

Elizabeth shook her head. The ways of the Ministry were already strange, but they seemed to get stranger.

"What else?" she asked.

"That's all. Whether this is the end of the matter I don't know. And neither, I suspect, does he. But I should imagine that if they had any plans for redevelopment they would hardly give the work of construction to a firm like Henderson and Speirs in Auchtarne. It would go to one of the big boys."

"Have you any idea why they're doing this?"

"Again one can only speculate. It is difficult to fathom the minds of the Defence Ministry. I would suspect that whatever they have built there has now become obsolete and therefore useless to them. The original agreement between Glendarroch Estates and the Crown land people specified that in the event of them withdrawing from the site they would leave it in the same condition as they found it."

"And that would apply to the Ministry of Defence too?"

"Probably."

"But you mean that it might well be that further building could take place there later?"

"If the Ministry wished to do so. On the other hand, if they return it to the Crown I think we can rest assured that there will be no further building. If they keep it to themselves, anything could happen."

"And probably will," said Elizabeth gloomily.

"I rather gather that the work will not take long," said George. "I understand from one or two things that Speirs let slip that there isn't much to be done to return the place to nature. So you will not, in the Scots phrase, have to thole these two young men who seem to have raised your hackles so much for very long."

"How long is not very long?"

"Perhaps four weeks."

"And they've already been there for more than one."

"So I believe."

"Could they not simply leave it?" asked Elizabeth. It was a relief to think that those two young men would not be there for evermore, but at the same time the thought of pile drivers breaking the peace and quiet of Glendarroch House was something which she didn't relish very much.

"For one thing they have to leave the site as they found it if they are giving it up, and if they are not giving it up, I presume the present buildings would have to be replaced. Even if they intend to keep the land and do nothing with it in the foreseeable future, they would probably be unwilling to leave the buildings for any Tom, Dick or Harry to break into and look round."

"I just hate the idea of any activity at Laird's Point. It's too close to the house, and I remember the trouble we had there before in the days when David Blair was here."

"I know. But I must remind you, Elizabeth, that you carry no weight in this matter at all. The land is not yours And they are legally entitled to access to Laird's Point across your land. I sincerely hope you are not thinking of lining that access with tin tacks to make it inconvenient to use."

"The thought hadn't crossed my mind till you mentioned it, George."

"Then I wish I had held my tongue."

"So I will just have to grin and bear these insufferable boors near my property."

"I fear so. But unless you go near them they are unlikely to bother you. As I understand it they had been there for a week before the sight of a lorryload of materials heading for the site alerted you to their presence."

"That's true."

"Then leave them alone. And they will leave you alone. It will not be for long. Live and let live, Elizabeth. It's not a bad motto to take to your heart."

6

Brian was just putting his boots on at the back door when Isabel appeared from the shop.

"Brian."

"Aye?"

"There's someone asking for you."

He could tell by her expression that whoever it was it was someone she didn't approve of, but as the person in question was following pretty close behind her she wasn't able to give vocal expression to her feelings.

"I'll leave you. There's a lot of folk in," she said, looking at the newcomer with some reservation, and she returned through the kitchen to the shop.

Brian straightened up and looked at the man who had followed her. He found his mind hurled back a distance of about four years. Back to the time he was trying his best to forget but which he never could.

"Joe MacMorran," he said, not with great pleasure.

"Got it in wan, Brian, got it in wan," said Joe, coming forward, a broad grin splitting his normally sullen features. He held out a hand and Brian took it with some reluctance, and found a firm grip and a hard shake.

"Man, it's good to see ye again," said Joe. "I often wondered what had happened to ye after ye got oot."

"I came home," said Brian simply, and then, to try to steer the conversation away from a painful area, he went on: "What are you doing here, Joe?"

"Got a joab," said Joe. "With Henderson and Speirs. Oot at Laird's Point. Demolition joab. Should last another two weeks, anyway."

The question had to be asked.

"You going straight, Joe?"

"Of course I'm going straight. A mug's game to do anything else, eh?"

"*I* know that. But I'm surprised to hear *you* say it."

"Learnt my lesson, Brian. Learnt it the hard way. No, no. I've a good joab and I've no complaints. I've my wee brother with me too. Stevie. Ye mind of him? He came on visiting days whiles."

Brian vaguely remembered a younger brother, but usually on those occasions he only had time for his own visitor—Isabel.

"Funny we should end up in the same place, eh?" said Joe. "I minded ye came from Glendarroch, so when I got the joab I thought I'd look ye up. See how ye were making oot."

"I'm making out fine, Joe."

"Glad to hear it."

"How long have you been here?"

"Just a week now. Travel over from Auchtarne on the ferry every morning. Back every evening. That's why I havena had the chance to look ye up before now."

"What makes today so different then?"

"Och, well, I'm the gaffer. I can start a wee bit later if I want to. Special privileges, see?"

Brian wondered why, if there were special privileges, and Joe had been so keen to see him, he hadn't exercised those privileges before now, rather than wait a week.

"What do ye do with yourself in a place like this, Brian?"

"It's not easy. But I'm fixed nicely now. A friend and I have gone into the peat cutting business. Seems to be going all right, too."

"Peat cutting? D'ye tell me? Do people still burn peat? I thought that went oot with Bonny Prince Charlie."

"There's a big market for peat and there are peat haggs on the hill at the back there. Plenty to be cut and dried."

He glanced at his watch. It was getting on and Ken would be waiting at the haggs to get started. But it wasn't easy to drag himself away from Joe MacMorran without seeming unnecessarily rude. And Joe showed no signs of wanting to let him go. He began questioning Brian about Glendarroch, what there was to do here, whether the tourist season was a busy one, what attracted them, and Brian found himself answering these questions with a growing reluctance because he couldn't quite see why they were being asked. Joe MacMorran wasn't the sort of person to be interested in tourism and the various activities connected with it, nor in the rather slow and humdrum lives which the locals lived in Glendarroch, and Brian kept looking for a motive behind all this, wondering what Joe was planning. Because he knew Joe of old. He had been a rebel, a morose communist with a chip on his shoulder who saw all the so-called rights and privileges other people had as rightfully belonging to himself.

But Joe had said that he was going straight, and the fact that he had a job as foreman on the demolition site at Laird's Point seemed to confirm that. Though that was by no means certain. Joe might simply be working because he needed money. There wasn't any other reason why he should want to work.

Demolition at Laird's Point, thought Brian with a slightly twisted smile. Good heavens, the Ministry of Defence establishment at Laird's Point had been set up by his own brother David who had started the whole thing rolling while he was here conducting a crusade to prove Brian innocent of the murder charge which had sent him to prison for ten years, during which time he had met Joe MacMorran. It was indeed a small world. And David had had the double disappointment of finding himself removed from the Ministry of Defence project just at the time it was reaching the stage of practical development, and of finding that his brother had indeed committed the murder which he was trying to prove him innocent of.

After about ten minutes, during which Joe had been uncharacteristically expansive and friendly, quite unlike the Joe he remembered in Barlinnie, Brian excused himself and said he would be late for work.

"Of course, Brian. Sorry. I wasna thinking. We'll have to meet some time. Maybe in Auchtarne, eh? Have a pint or two and talk over old times."

"Of course," said Brian, making a mental note to be prepared with an excuse if and when that invitation became more specific.

With many expressions of goodwill, Joe departed round the side of the shop and Brian stood looking after him thoughtfully. There was something jaunty in Joe's walk, something false in his attitude, but for the life of him Brian couldn't understand why, or what Joe was trying to do.

"Who was that, Brian?"

Isabel had come to stand beside him as he watched Joe go and, feeling a sudden need for her support, he put a hand on her shoulder.

"Someone I knew," he said.

"In—there?" asked Isabel. It was her usual way of referring to those lost years.

He nodded.

"I didn't like him," she said.

"I'm not all that keen on him myself," said Brian.

"What did he want?"

"Just to talk over old times as far as I can make out," said Brian. "He suggested we meet again for a pint in Auchtarne."

"Are you going?"

He knew that non-committal tone of voice. If he said yes, Isabel would remain non-committal.

"No," he said.

And as he knew she would she smiled her relief.

"What's he doing here?"

"Working at Laird's Point. A demolition job."

"Demolition? Well, that's one good thing come out of his visit. We know what's happening at Laird's Point now. I wonder Mrs Mack hadn't got wind of it earlier."

"That's right. Don't worry. I don't want anything to do with him. He's not my type."

"I'm glad to hear it. But are you his?"

"Eh?"

"Why did he come to find you?"

"He knew I was here."

"Were you friendly with him in—there?"

"No. Hardly spoke to him."

"Well, what does he want?"

"I don't know. And that worries me. I feel I ought to know."

"Well, don't try to find out if it means getting close to him."

He squeezed her shoulder and kissed her forehead.

"See you later, love," he said and turned to the van.

As he drove up to the peat haggs he couldn't get Joe MacMorran out of his mind. There were several things that worried him. First was the fact which had worried him from the beginning: that Joe was working. But after some thought he realised that there might well be an explanation for that. Speirs of Henderson and Speirs was a shady character. He was probably employing Joe and paying him cash so that there was no record for tax and national insurance payments and Joe would still be able to draw unemployment benefit at home in Glasgow. If Joe's financial circumstances were the same as they used to be such an arrangement might suit him very well, especially if the job was only for a few weeks. But second, and more puzzling, was the fact that Joe had wasted about an hour and a half walking from Laird's Point to the Glendarroch Store, having an apparently pointless chat with him and then walking back again. He couldn't see the reason for it. Joe wouldn't worry too much about taking time off from a job. But the fact that he had done so to so little purpose was odd. He had a feeling that there was always a reason behind everything that Joe MacMorran did. And it worried him that there didn't seem to be one.

7

Stevie couldn't for the life of him understand what this place had ever been used for. He played the torch round the bare concrete walls of the underground complex of Laird's Point and tried to picture what purpose it might have served. There were three interconnected chambers, very small and cramped, with no access to the outside world except through the main entrance door which stood at the end of a concrete passage and a turning flight of stairs. Probably at one time there had been an intention to put equipment of some kind round the walls, but the equipment had evidently never been installed. There was no sign of anchorage points having been used, and there was certainly no moveable equipment left in the place.

Well, it didn't matter. Tomorrow they would start pulling this place apart, dynamiting the curiously thick concrete walls, reducing it to rubble so that natural growth would take over on the surface. Before many weeks had passed the area would return to the wild from which it had been built and no one would ever wonder what had happened at Laird's Point again.

"Stevie!"

Joe's voice from the top of the stairs echoed round the empty chambers, startling Stevie with its suddenness after the silence which had enveloped him for so long.

"Aye, Joe," he shouted.

"What are ye doing doon there?"

"Just looking."

"Well, stoap looking and come away up here. There's work to be done, my lad."

Stevie left the underground complex with a last glance round and made his way up to the surface again, switching off the torch as the beam grew pale in the growing daylight.

Joe stood waiting for him, his face lit with unholy glee.

"I've got it, Stevie," he said.

"Got what?"

"Something to kick the lady laird in the bread-basket with. Come oan."

"What are ye thinking of, Joe?"

"I'll tell ye, I'll tell ye. Later, though. We'll get her sorted oot tonight."

And he would say no more at that point. For the rest of the day he treated Stevie and the others in the gang with a boisterous joviality, but drove them hard, and Stevie didn't like it very much at all. He knew the signs. Joe was working on one of his hare-brained schemes again.

At knocking-off time Joe dismissed the other four and sent them off to the ferry, but he stayed behind himself and told Stevie to stay with him.

"How are we going to get back to Auchtarne, Joe?" Stevie asked. "That's the last ferry over tonight."

"We're no going back by the ferry, Stevie."

"Then how—?"

"We'll walk."

"Eh? But it must be getting on for ten miles—!"

"Aye. Do ye good. Ye're getting fat, sonny."

And he laughed loudly and slapped Stevie on the back, making him wince.

"A good night's walk'll do ye good," he said.

"A night's walk—?"

"Aye. Come oan. It's time we got ready."

He marched across the open ground and Stevie followed

D.I.T.G.—B

him with some reluctance. He knew Joe in this sort of mood, knew that there was some wild and probably impractical scheme running round in his head, knew that the kind of person the lady laird was was the kind Joe hated above all others so that whatever he had in mind would be correspondingly violent. Yet what could he do? Joe was a dangerous man to cross, as Stevie had found several times in the past to his cost. Maybe if he could suggest caution it might cool the fire in Joe. But he doubted it.

Joe was detaching the bunch of keys from his waist belt as he headed for one of the concrete blockhouses. Not the blockhouse they used as their office. It was another one, set further away, safely apart from the rest.

He reached the door and began to fit the key into the padlock which kept it firmly shut. Stevie swallowed, the first ripples of genuine fear stirring in his gut. He knew what this blockhouse contained. So would anyone else, of course, for on the door, stencilled in recent and rather amateurish letters were the words:

CAUTION—NO SMOKING—NO NAKED FLAMES

And underneath was a crudely drawn skull and cross-bones.

8

Sleep came early to Alice but not to Bob. Yet he was content in his sleeplessness. It had been a hard day, out in the cold of mid-March from the first grey streaking of dawn till after the short gloaming had sunk into night. He should have gone out like a light as usual, but not tonight. He listened to Alice's regular breathing beside him and he smiled in contentment. Normally on the rare occasions when sleep evaded him he found himself lying getting tenser and tenser, more and more determined to get to sleep and consequently getting further and further away from achieving it.

Not tonight, though. Tonight was a night of pleasant thoughts.

Alice, he thought. She had come back to him. Complete-ly and utterly. The awful mental scar caused by losing the

baby and knowing there could be no more had finally
healed, and as though on cue the cot in the next room
creaked as wee Donald turned over in his sleep. To
Donald Alice was mother, the only mother he had ever
known since Dougal's wife Amy had died giving birth to
him. And now to Alice Donald was her son. Bob was
content that it should be so. Sometimes there were deep
and perhaps bitter regrets that he would never be a father
himself, but they were fleeting regrets, soon dispersed by
practical things, like watching Alice tending Donald and
seeing the maternal instinct satisfied in her.

He put his hands behind his head and stared at the
invisible ceiling. Around them the March night held the
cottage in total darkness and silence and peace.

Life was really very good. More responsibility on the
estate, gamekeeper now as well as water bailiff. An
important member of the little community which made up
Glendarroch . . .

Heaviness crept over him and he let it come, knowing
that sleep was beginning to take over, and accepting it half
regretfully as it meant the end of these pleasant reflec-
tions. His eyes closed . . .

And then suddenly he was sitting bolt upright in bed,
heart pounding with the shock of surprise. *What was that?*

Briefly he thought it was one of those occasions when
something jerks you violently awake just as you are
dropping into a deep sleep. A little frightening, certainly
annoying, but nothing more.

But it wasn't that, for Alice was sitting up beside him,
and from the next room came the first cry from Donald,
startled into wakefulness as well.

"What was that?"

Alice's voice, thick with sleep, echoed his own thought.

"An explosion . . ."

It fell into place. There had been a bang. Not all that
loud, probably some distance away, but loud enough in
the total silence of this part of the world.

Alice switched on the bedlight and he blinked blearily
at his watch on the bedside table. Ten minutes past one . .

He flung back the bedclothes and shivered as the cold
of the night hit him.

Alice got out the other side and went through to the

next room, pulling on her dressing gown, and as Bob
dressed he heard her speaking soothingly to Donald,
calming him down. After a moment or two the crying
stopped and Alice appeared in the bedroom again with a
tousled and sleepy Donald in her arms.

"What was that, Bob?"

"An explosion. And that only means one thing . . ."

He struggled into his boots and seized his pullover,
heading for the door.

"Are you sure? It wasn't thunder maybe. . . ?"

"Not the weather for thunder."

He kissed her and rumpled Donald's hair and then
slipped into his anorak.

"I'll be back," he said.

She stared at him with worry in her eyes. She knew
what an explosion here meant as well as he did himself.

"Take care," she said.

"Don't worry."

And he tugged open the front door, gasping in the
sudden chill of the night and shrugging deeper into his
anorak as he ran towards the land-rover standing in the
outhouse at the back.

9

Grimly Dougal took two cartridges and put one in each
barrel of the shotgun.

"You be careful with that thing, now," said Grace.

"Of course I'll be careful, Mother. Go back to bed."

"I'm telling you, you'd be better without it."

"If there's poachers out there I'm not going to ask for
trouble."

"You'll likely get it anyway."

"Aye. Likely."

"Anyway, what would poachers be doing up here?"

"That explosion wasn't up here. It's the hills. They bring
the sound round. Like an echo, sort of. It was nearer the
Taylors'."

"Then Bob will deal with it."

"If they're using explosives Bob'll need help."

"What would they be doing with explosives at this time

of year?"

"Mining the salmon pools, of course."

"There are no salmon in the river just now."

Dougal paused with his hand on the door latch.

"You're right," he said thoughtfully.

"So it was probably thunder," said Grace with an air of satisfaction and went to fill the kettle as though everything was settled and Dougal would now put away his gun and return to bed after a cup of tea.

"That was no thunder, Mother," he said. "I know thunder when I hear it. And I know an explosion when I hear it too."

"It might have been one of those aeroplanes breaking the sound fence or whatever it is they call it."

"Och, Mother, away you go."

And he went himself, leaving Grace with the kettle in her hand.

It was pitch dark outside after the light in the croft house and he had to use his torch to get to the barn where the land-rover was housed.

But before he reached it he stood in the yard and tried to orientate himself. He had been sound asleep when the explosion had happened and being jerked out of such a sleep made it very difficult to work out exactly where the sound had come from. And the way sound rolled round these hills of Ardvain made it doubly difficult. He closed his eyes and tried to think back to what he had heard, to re-establish every last detail of what had woken him.

His head turned. *There*. He had been right. Down towards the Taylors' cottage, but not quite so far, and then across to where the river Darroch dropped in a series of shallows and pools towards the loch. Somewhere in that direction. He could take the land-rover across the rough ground to the point where the river dropped in a cataract from the high fall of Poacher's Drop and beyond which the salmon could not go. It was little more than a burn at this point, widening from there on as the waters from tiny runnels joined it on its journey.

Having established in his own mind where he wanted to head, Dougal put the shotgun carefully on the passenger seat of the land-rover, climbed into the driver's seat and started the engine.

The headlights cut two brilliant swathes through the darkness and Dougal swung round out of the yard and up to the track.

Behind him he sensed the kitchen curtain twitch aside as his mother watched him go.

As the land-rover bounced and lurched its way along the track Dougal felt a dull sense of resentment. He hated poachers with the crofter's deep and bitter hatred for those who are prepared to take the painstaking work of a man in the crudest possible way, but even in that resentment there was puzzlement too. His mother was right. Although an explosion meant that someone somewhere was mining a river or pool to concuss the fish so that they floated to the surface and were easily gathered for a quick getaway, this was, as Grace had said, the wrong time of year. There were no salmon in the river in March. They would not begin their run to the spawning grounds for a couple of months yet. So why. . . ?

Unless they were fools. Dougal's opinion of the average poacher's intelligence was not high. They came up from Glasgow, a city which seemed to Dougal to be the last place on earth anyone would want to live in, they knew little of the cycle of life in the country, they cared even less about the need to conserve that cycle so that there was continuity, and they were quite likely to make elementary and basic mistakes of that kind. He had a great respect for their cunning and ruthlessness but not for their knowledge of the product they were planning to steal. So it was more than possible that they had got the time of year wrong, and that they were even now standing hopefully on the bank of the Darroch waiting for the fish to float to the surface, not realising that they would never appear. And if they stayed there for long enough, he might be in time to clobber one or two of them, an action which would give him an enormous amount of pleasure.

He stopped to open the gate at the rutted track which led towards the rocky outfall where the young river dropped into its first proper runnel, then drove on slowly, the springs of the land-rover creaking and groaning in protest, until he reached the edge where he stopped, switched off the engine and extinguished the lights. He sat for a minute waiting for his eyes to grow accustomed to the darkness, before picking up the shotgun and stepping out of the land-rover. He closed the door quietly and stood listening.

There was no sound except for the slight ticking of the engine as it cooled.

The sky was bright with stars and there was a thin sickle of moon over the shoulder of Ben Darroch, enough to give a little light, and Dougal, knowing this ground like the back of his hand, began to move down the side of the incipient river, the shotgun crooked in his arm.

The river meandered over rough ground, occasionally running into a wide deep pool and then continuing downwards in its inevitable course. After a quarter of a mile it entered a stand of trees and in their shelter the light grew very dim and Dougal had to slow his pace. Every tree trunk could hide a man, every shadow could be a threat.

He stopped and listened but could hear nothing except the steady splashing of the river as it chuckled over its stones to his right. And then in the edge of his vision a shadow moved. He swung round, levelling the shotgun and his finger sought the trigger.

"Dougal!"

The voice was a hoarse whisper and Dougal let out his breath in a quiet whistle.

"Bob—you scared the daylights out of me," he breathed.

"You heard it?"

"Aye. Where are they?"

"I don't know. I've seen no sign. Don't even know which side of the river they're on."

"I began at Poacher's Drop. They'll not be higher than that."

"So they must be below. But which side?"

"You take the other side. I'll stay here. I'll meet you at the Minister's Pool."

"Right."

Brief words, but a perfect understanding.

Bob melted away into the shadows and Dougal listened for the change in tone of the river as the flow of water was altered by Bob's boots crossing over. Then he began to follow the course of the river downwards through the trees.

Out into the open again and there was Bob's shadowy figure much clearer on the other side. He saw Bob raise a hand in acknowledgement and he did the same. Then they both concentrated on the rough ground stretching down to the next block of woodland which lay another quarter of a mile below.

Dougal's side of the river was the easier one here and he made better progress than Bob. As he reached the fringe of the next wood he glanced back and saw him a hundred yards or so behind. He plunged on into the undergrowth and once again the moon and the starlight faded into almost total darkness.

He was getting impatient now. Time was passing and with every minute it was more likely that the poachers would give up their fruitless search and leave. That would be all right in one sense because at least they would be leaving empty-handed, but unless they got one hell of a fright they would come back and next time they might be a great deal luckier than they had been this. He increased his pace through the broken blanket of last year's undergrowth. There was no point in trying to maintain silence. There had been a long frosty spell and the undergrowth was brittle. You couldn't move without sounding like a herd of elephants, especially when you couldn't see where you were putting your feet.

Just ahead was Peddie's Pool, named after the old laird, Sir Logan Peddie, Mrs Cunningham's father. Dougal remembered when he was very young seeing the old man, an ancient pair of boots enclosing a disgraceful old pair of corduroy trousers with an out-at-elbows tweed jacket and an ancient hat stuck on his head, contentedly puffing a foul old pipe as he cast again and again into this pool. And he remembered some of the fish he had taken from it. Great big salmon that made the young Dougal's eyes boggle, and there had been the memorable day when the old man had thrust a fish nearly as big Dougal himself into his arms, saying "Take that to your parents young Dougal. I'm sick of eating the things." And there had been the time when a new assistant keeper had caught the old man fishing the pool, looking like a tramp as usual, and had tried to take him away to the police station at Auchtarne for poaching, and only the arrival of Crawford the old ghillie had convinced the young man of his appalling mistake, and Sir Logan had given the man ten shillings for undertaking his work so zealously . . .

It was an odd time to find reminiscences flooding his mind, but that was the effect that Peddie's Pool had on him. It was a wide deep expanse of still water with overhanging banks where the salmon lay in summer and where there was often good fishing, for the trees were drawn back here, leaving plenty of room for a cast.

Dougal approached the Pool, his eyes scanning the open ground ahead in the better light.

And there they were. Two of them. Shadowy figures on the bank, crouched and staring at the still waters.

Waiting for the fish, thought Dougal contemptuously as a savage thrill of triumph spread through him.

They must have heard his approach at the same time as he caught sight of them, for they leapt to their feet and began to run in the opposite direction, heading for the shelter of the trees again.

"Stop where you are!" shouted Dougal. "Bob—they're here!"

He heard an answering shout from the opposite bank some distance behind him, but the two figures showed no sign of obeying his order. He brought the shotgun up to his shoulder.

"Stop or I'll fire!" he shouted.

The leading figure sped on, but the one behind stopped and turned. He was just at the fringe of the trees and another couple of paces would have taken him out of Dougal's view. Distance was difficult to judge in this light. Possibly fifty, maybe sixty yards away . . .

Dougal saw the dim figure's hand go down to his pocket.

My God, he's armed, he thought . . . They had used explosives. He ought to have reckoned that they would have more than explosives . . . The hand was coming up . . .

Dougal pulled the nearer trigger and there was a loud report. The figure at the fringe of the trees staggered, tried to run and then sagged to the ground.

As it did so Bob burst through the trees behind Dougal, having forded the river slightly higher up in time to see the man go down.

"What are you doing, Dougal?" he asked.

Dougal lowered the shotgun, feeling his hands trembling.

"He had a gun. He was going for a gun," he said.

Bob stared at him in the dim light of moon and stars and what Dougal saw in his eyes was not at all encouraging.

"You'd better give me that," said Bob, holding out his hand, and without a word of protest Dougal handed him the gun.

Bob took it and turned to head for the fallen figure.

"I just hope for your sake you haven't killed him, Dougal," he said.

Chapter Two

1

Dr Wallace looked down thoughtfully at the young man lying on the bed. He had propped pillows under his legs to raise them and he had bound them firmly. There was little more he could do till the ambulance came, but the man did not seem to be in too much pain. The wounds would need debridement and it was possible at one place where there was a severe laceration that a skin graft might be necessary. It was a good thing that Dougal had shot low. Had the wounds been higher it might have been a very different story.

He passed a hand wearily across his forehead and looked across at the other man in the chair beside the bed, who glowered back at him resentfully as though it were he who had shot his brother.

"I'll leave you with him," said Wallace. "He'll be all right till the ambulance gets here."

"No thanks to that bastard through there," muttered the one in the chair.

Wallace looked dubious and the man seemed to take it as criticism.

"I tell you, we were just having a quiet walk through the woods," he said.

"At one o'clock on a March morning?" said Wallace disbelievingly, and he left the room and returned to the living room of the croft house. He closed the door quietly and surveyed the three people there. Grace was, as usual, presiding over a tea pot, her universal remedy for all ills, and no bad one at that, though he doubted whether a tea pot would do much for the young man on the bed. Bob stood in front of the fire, his hands in his pockets, a worried frown on his face. And Dougal sat at the table, nursing a cup of tea in his hands.

"How is he?" asked Bob.

"He'll live," said Wallace and went and sat down beside Dougal. "You know I'm going to have to report this to the police, Dougal," he said gently.

Dougal nodded.

"I expect you will, doctor," he said.

"The man must go to hospital and they'll report it if I don't. The police don't like gunshot wounds. Neither do hospitals."

"What do you think will happen, Doctor?" asked Grace. Wallace shrugged.

"I've no idea," he said. "That's not for me to say. The man's injuries are mercifully slight and he should be out of hospital in a couple of days, unless they need to do a skin graft, in which case he may be there for a fortnight. But it could have been a lot worse."

"I shot deliberately low," said Dougal.

"Just as well."

"I told you not to take that gun with you," said Grace accusingly.

"And if I hadn't they'd have got clean away, wouldn't they?" said Dougal.

There was a short silence.

"I'm not regretting it, you know," said Dougal defiantly. "I'd do it again if I had to."

Wallace nodded.

"I can understand your feelings in the circumstances, Dougal," he said. "But I've got a nasty feeling you may have a little more difficulty getting understanding from the police and the procurator fiscal."

"I thought he had a gun."

"I know," said Wallace. "That would make it self defence. If you can prove it."

"I don't have to prove anything. It's them that have to prove they were just out for a quiet walk, like they say they were."

"I know that seems highly unlikely, but it is possible."

Grace brought him a cup of tea and he took it. It was hot and strong. He watched as she took another cup to Bob who simply shook his head and smiled at her briefly.

Outside the throb of an engine grew in the silence of the still-dark morning, and headlights swept the living room curtains.

"That'll be the ambulance," said Wallace and Bob headed for the door.

The ambulancemen came in with a stretcher and Wallace conducted them through to the bedroom and watched while they transferred the young man with practised ease from the bed to the stretcher and began to negotiate the narrow door of the bedroom with it.

The other man rose slowly to his feet and followed without a word or a glance at Wallace. His face was set and tense. A dangerous customer, that one, thought Wallace.

He followed, and was in time to see the older man stop and look at Dougal. He whispered something to him very quietly and Wallace wasn't sure if he'd heard the words correctly. But they sounded something like, "I'll get you for this."

Then he followed the ambulancemen and the stretcher out into the yard.

There was a pre-dawn chill in the air and, glancing at his watch, Wallace saw that it was after five o'clock. Bob, Dougal and Grace followed him out, Grace having put a coat on over her dressing gown.

"Don't you stand out here getting cold," he said and she nodded but made no attempt to go in.

It was a strangely silent party which watched as the back doors of the ambulance closed behind the two brothers, the two ambulancemen got into the cab and the vehicle moved slowly and carefully away towards the rough track which wound down the hillside to Glendarroch. It would be a bumpy and uncomfortable journey to the cottage hospital at Auchtarne, but there was nothing else for it.

Wallace turned and went back into the croft house to retrieve his bag and the others followed him in. There was a reticence about them, he thought, as though they knew something had gone wrong somewhere but they were going to stick together over it. And that was probably exactly right. They would stick together. They might, perhaps, argue among themselves that Dougal should never have fired the shotgun, but they would present a united front to the world.

And Wallace was not quite sure where his own sympathies ought to lie.

2

"I'll just take a box of matches, Isabel. What those scouts do with the cooker in the hall I don't know. It's covered in used matches."

Isabel hid a smile, took the money from Mrs Mack and put it in the till. Every time Mrs Mack came in and bought nothing but a box of matches Isabel knew that she either wanted information or wished to impart it. She waited, and it wasn't for long.

Mrs Mack's face became portentous and even more solemn than usual.

"You'll have heard about the mad crofter, Isabel," she said.

Isabel blinked.

"The mad crofter?" she echoed. "No, I don't think I have, Mrs Mack."

"Dougal Lachlan," said Mrs Mack in the tone of voice of someone using a dirty word for the first time.

"What about Dougal?"

"You'll never guess what he's been up to now," said Mrs Mack as though whatever it was it was only the climax to a long career of villainy and loose living.

"I'm quite sure I won't," Isabel agreed.

Mrs Mack was spinning it out a bit, because at the moment the shop was empty and it would have a better effect if there were a few people around to hear what she had to impart and to benefit from her moral judgement on whatever it was.

"He's shot someone," said Mrs Mack.

"Nonsense," said Isabel immediately.

"Shot someone," Mrs Mack repeated with evident satisfaction. "A young man who never did anyone any harm. Shot him last night. With his shotgun," she added to drive home the point. "The man's in the Auchtarne cottage hospital with severe gunshot wounds and he is not expected to recover."

Her eyes were alight with enthusiastic disapproval and Isabel began to feel worried. Many of Mrs Mack's pronouncements, she knew, arose from her strong but misdirected sense of moral duty, and frequently they were based on a totally wrong assessment of a situation, but here there seemed to be too much circumstantial evidence to dismiss the whole thing out of hand. Perhaps there was some truth in the matter after all.

"Why did he shoot him?" she asked.

The light in Mrs Mack's eyes died out. Isabel had asked her the one question she had no answer to. At the moment. Though undoubtedly the time would come.

"I'm sure I don't know," she said in the tone of voice which implied that actually knowing might be regarded as a sin. "But it's my belief that the man is off his head and probably has been ever since his wife died. Living alone away up at Ardvain there must have a terrible effect on a man's sanity."

Isabel hid another smile. Dougal had his faults, she knew, but it was hard to imagine anyone with his feet more firmly planted on the ground and a less likely subject for insanity she found it hard to imagine.

"If Dougal has shot someone he will have had his reasons. He's had trouble up there with poachers before now."

She remembered very clearly how Mr Murdoch had once nearly got peppered with shot from Dougal and he had been very careful to look for his accidental pheasants in a different direction ever since. She didn't mention this fact to Mrs Mack. It might not have gone down too well.

"What is there to poach at this time of year?" asked Mrs Mack triumphantly. "No, Isabel. No one in their senses would go poaching just now. I truly believe that man has finally taken leave of his senses and should be certified. The trouble is that ever since Mrs Cunningham put him in charge of that deer farm he has become totally unmanageable. I knew that was a mistake and I would have told Mrs Cunningham so if she hadn't appointed him so quickly. He has taken to living by the gun. And as my Mr Mack used to always say those that live by the gun shall perish by the gun."

"I thought it was by the sword," said Isabel mildly.

"The same thing. You mark my words, Isabel, once a man gets a taste for such things it is not long before he starts wearing jackboots and a swastika."

Isabel tried to imagine Dougal dressed up in Nazi uniform but found it difficult. Evidently her imagination was not as vivid as Mrs Mack's.

"Where did this happen?" she asked.

"I'm not sure."

"And when?"

"In the small hours. About two o'clock, I believe. And Dr Wallace was called out to attend to the man and an ambulance came to rush him to the hospital and there was an emergency operation but they don't think it will be successful. God moves in a mysterious way," she added irrelevantly. "But I shall expect a lot of activity from the police very shortly, Isabel. And the first action I shall expect is that they will take that man's gun licence away."

"I doubt if they can revoke a firearms certificate just like that," Isabel objected. "Not until the trial and not until he's proved guilty."

"We shall see. We shall hear more of this, Isabel, you mark my words. We haven't heard the end of it by a long chalk."

Mrs Mack rattled the matchbox as though to make sure it was sufficiently full, thrust it into her shopping basket and marched out of the shop with an air of determination as though she were about to set off for Ardvain to demand the surrender of Dougal's firearms certificate herself.

Isabel stared thoughtfully after her retreating figure. Something told her that it was not all blethers, that there was a central core of truth in what she said. The trouble with Mrs Mack was that you were never sure just how far that central core extended. Sometimes it was very small. At others it was surprisingly large.

But Isabel had a strong feeling that Dougal Lachlan might be in for quite a bit of trouble.

3

Sergeant Murray sat bolt upright in the chair beside the desk, his face impassive as he looked at Bob and Dougal.

"I have spoken to the injured man this morning," he said.

"How is he?" Elizabeth asked.

"He is in some discomfort, but no danger, I'm told," said

Murray.

"I'm glad of that."

"Indeed, it is a good thing," the Sergeant agreed. "I have also had a report from Dr Wallace and from the hospital regarding his injuries. They were caused by a shotgun."

"Aye. It was my shotgun," said Dougal dourly.

"It was, was it?"

"It was."

"And was it you that fired it?"

"Right again."

"I see." Sergeant Murray rubbed a hand over his chin as though he were slightly puzzled, though no puzzlement appeared in his face. Elizabeth realised suddenly that the Sergeant was embarrassed. It was a difficult position for him. He knew Dougal personally. Had known him for a long time, probably admired and respected him for all the many qualities of honesty and straightforwardness which Dougal possessed. And now, through the responsibilities of his job, he was forced to treat Dougal like a possible criminal when she knew, and he knew as well, Dougal had probably been doing no more than his duty.

"I have to tell you that the man says that he and his brother were simply walking back to Auchtarne, had got lost taking what they thought was a short cut through the woods, and suddenly found themselves confronted by a man with a shotgun. They took fright and ran, whereupon the man with the shotgun fired and hit the younger man, Stephen MacMorran."

"Have they identified the man who fired the gun, Sergeant?" asked Elizabeth, seeing a sudden slight ray of hope.

"They have not, Mrs Cunningham. They have not yet been asked to identify Dougal, but that is not relevant. Dougal has admitted here that he fired the gun at Stephen MacMorran. There is no doubt about that."

Dougal was uttering contemptuous grunts.

"And you believe all that havering, Sergeant?" he said. "About walking back to Auchterne from Glendarroch at after one o'clock in the morning and taking a short cut which would add five miles to their journey over some of the roughest ground outside the heights?"

Sergeant Murray shrugged.

"It's not a question of what I believe, Dougal. It's a question of what I am told in a statement, signed by the man who makes it. And that is what he said. Forebye, his brother Joseph MacMorran confirms it. And the chiels are from Glasgow. It is doubtful if they would know which direction a short cut was taking them in."

"Then they'd be daft to try any short cut at all, wouldn't they?"

"Indeed, that is probably very true, but townsfolk do funny things when they aren't very sure."

He made a note in his notebook and then looked up at Bob.

"I'd like to hear from you what happened last night," he said. "Not what you think happened. What you know happened. What you saw yourself and what you heard yourself."

Elizabeth watched Bob as he explained how he had been woken by what was evidently an explosion, that a glance at his watch had shown the time to be ten past one in the morning, how Alice and wee Donald had also been woken by it, how he had dressed and taken the land-rover to the river.

"Why would you be taking the land-rover to the river?" asked Sergeant Murray.

"Because an explosion at that time of night means just one thing. Poachers," said Bob.

Murray looked dubious.

"At this time of the year? It is the close season for poaching."

"Aye. You know that and I know that and everyone who lives in Glendarroch and Auchtarne knows that, but do folk from outside? From the towns? You'd be surprised what some of them get up to in their ignorance, Murray."

"I'm sure, I'm sure," said Murray soothingly, for Bob had become a little heated. "So what happened then?"

Bob took a deep breath before going on to tell how he had reached the river and nearly bumped into Dougal which had all but given him a heart attack and how the two of them had bracketed the river. How his side of the river had been rougher ground and how on the approach to Peddie's Pool Dougal had been a hundred yards or so ahead of him.

"Then what happened?" asked Murray as Bob paused.

"I was just about entering the wood when I heard Dougal shout. He was asking for help. I stopped for a moment to pinpoint where he was. It sounded about fifty yards ahead and on the opposite bank, of course, but I couldn't see anything because of the trees and bushes and the light was very poor in there."

"Aye?"

"I started to ford the river and when I was nearly at the other side Dougal shouted again. I began to run. Got water over the top of my boots too—"

"Never mind that. Go on."

"Then I heard a shot."

Bob said it with some reluctance, as though by saying it he were condemning Dougal to a long term in prison which, Elizabeth thought, might be nearer the truth than any of them cared to contemplate.

Murray was quietly making notes. When Bob didn't resume his story he looked up.

"Mphm?" he said encouragingly.

"I reached Peddie's Pool. Dougal was standing on the bank with the shotgun in his hands. There was a smell of powder. And I got there just in time to see the man falling. I'm sorry, Dougal."

"What are you being sorry for? That's exactly what you did see," said Dougal impatiently.

"Anyway, I took the gun away from him. Just in case, you know . . ."

"In case of what?"

"In case of accidents. Any more accidents," said Bob.

"It wasn't an accident," said Dougal. "I shot him all right, and I don't see the point of all these damn silly questions. I've said I shot him. The man's injured. We did what we could for him and we carried him back to Ardvain and Bob called Dr Wallace and the other man came and helped us, though he wasn't exactly friendly. What else do you want to know?"

Murray turned to him.

"Why did you shoot him, Dougal?" he asked.

"Because I thought he had a gun."

Elizabeth heard Murray grunt. She wasn't sure but she thought it was a grunt of approval.

"What made you think that?" he asked.

Dougal frowned thoughtfully, trying to recall the events of last night.

"It was dark in there, to let you understand," he said slowly. "There was a moon and the stars were bright, but in the trees it was dark. Sort of light and shade. The branches and trunks made it difficult to get a clear picture. You know what I mean?"

Murray nodded.

"I know. Go on."

"Well, I found two men crouched at the edge of the pool. I could see them clearly, for the light was not bad there. They must have heard me or seen me just about the same time I saw them, for they began to run and that's when I called on them to stop and shouted to Bob. That's what Bob heard."

Murray nodded again.

"They didn't stop. Bob shouted back, but he was a wee bittie away and by that time they'd almost reached the trees. I shouted at them to stop again or else I'd fire. I didn't really mean it. At least, I don't think I did. But then one of them stopped and turned. Stopped right at the edge of the trees when another step or two would have taken him into cover. And as he turned his right hand went to his pocket."

"You're sure of that?" Murray interrupted.

"No, I'm not sure of anything, Sergeant. It was all so quick and the light was very bad, like I told you. But that's what I thought he was doing. And then his hand came out again and I thought, 'My God, he's got a gun'."

"Did you see a gun?"

"No, I didn't. But I knew they'd been using explosives so there wasn't much reason why they shouldn't have a gun as well, and I wasn't going to wait to find out if my eyes were playing me tricks or not, so I fired. I fired low on purpose, I think. I just wanted to stop him from firing at me."

Silence fell in the office again. From the reception room came the clatter of Lorna's typewriter and the occasional ring of the telephone. Out there the ordinary daily life of the estate was going on as if nothing had happened, but in here there was a tension such as Elizabeth had rarely known before.

Murray finished making notes and sat staring at what he had written for a while.

"I don't like it," he said at last.

"It's the truth," said Dougal indignantly.

"Oh, I'm not doubting that, Dougal," said Murray. "But I don't like the whole story. I have to look at it from both points of view, you understand. Now, these two men claim to have been taking an innocent walk, like I said. Let's see what there is to support your story. This explosion. Can you be sure it was an explosion?"

Bob and Dougal looked at each other.

"I know an explosion when I hear one," said Bob, and Dougal nodded agreement.

"I know that," said Murray, "but on your own admission it was the noise which woke you up. How can you be sure that a noise which you heard while you were actually asleep was what you assumed it to be? You see what I'm getting at? Could it not have been a clap of thunder, a sonic boom, something like that?"

"Havers," said Dougal. "They're completely different."

"I'm just trying to put into your minds what counsel is going to say in court," said Murray.

"You think it'll come to a court case, Sergeant?" asked Elizabeth.

"I don't think there's any doubt of that, Mrs Cunningham," said Murray apologetically. "I shall have to report to the procurator fiscal and it will be for him to decide whether to proceed with a charge, but to my mind there is no doubt that he will."

"But supposing—supposing these two men could be persuaded not to proceed with charges—"

"It's not up to them, Mrs Cunningham. One of them is in hospital with gunshot wounds. The matter has been reported to the police. The police have been asked to investigate and they will have to report to the procurator fiscal. It's up to him to decide what happens. Not the police. Not the two parties involved. That's the way it is."

Elizabeth sat back, suddenly feeling that things were slipping completely out of her control.

Murray rubbed his chin again.

"You see, the problem is that the men were not armed.

They had no firearm on their persons, and a search first thing this morning of the area round Peddie's Pool shows no trace of a firearm having been dropped or flung away by the man Stephen MacMorran."

"I thought he had one," said Dougal stubbornly.

"Aye, and if he had had one you'd have had plenty of justification," said Murray. "But as he hadn't your position is a little difficult."

"How long are you supposed to wait to find out whether you're going to be shot at or not?" demanded Dougal indignantly.

"That's a matter I don't think the courts have ever decided," said Murray.

"No, I bet they haven't," said Dougal. "Those judges and lawyers have probably never been in that position."

"Likely. But you see the point, Dougal. You have to have evidence to back up your story."

"What sort of evidence do you want?"

"If I were the procurator fiscal I would want to find a wee pistol with the man Stephen MacMorran's finger-prints on it, and preferably no one else's. And I'd want to find evidence that they had actually caused an explosion, whether at Peddie's Pool or elsewhere. Failing that I'd at least want to find evidence of a fish dead from concussion."

"But there are no fish in the river just now," said Bob despairingly.

"Exactly," said Murray. "And neither is there a pistol and neither is there a fuse or detonator or anything else."

"There must be something like that if they caused an explosion," said Elizabeth suddenly.

"Aye, but where, Mrs Cunningham? It's a big area. And it's an area where you can hide things like that very easily. Oh, we'll search, of course, to the best of our ability. But I wouldn't give much for our chances of success."

He stood up, pocketing his notebook and pulling down his uniform tunic.

"I shall be getting away now to prepare my report." He glanced at Dougal in some embarrassment. "I'm sorry Dougal, but there's nothing else I can do."

"I know," said Dougal. "I've told you the truth. There's nothing more I can do either."

"I appreciate that. Thank you. Good morning, Mrs

Cunningham. I'm sorry."

He went out and closed the door. They heard him say a few words to Lorna, and then the conversation ceased and Lorna's typewriter began again. It wasn't until they heard the sound of Murray's car engine fade down the drive that Elizabeth stirred herself.

"Its a mess," she said.

"Aye, it is," said Dougal with some bitterness. "Maybe I should just have shot the man dead. Then at least he couldn't have gone telling lies all over the place."

"You'd have had to shoot them both," said Bob.

"In any case," said Elizabeth, "I think you're going to need a lawyer, Dougal. That at least is something I can help you with."

4

It wasn't that there was one big pain, more a whole lot of tiny little irritations. Stevie shifted gingerly and uncomfortably in the neat bed, not letting his legs brush the cage which was set over them.

The ward was bright and cheerful and didn't seem like a ward at all, really. There were only six beds and one of them wasn't occupied. A mid-morning sun glanced through the high windows, giving no hint of the actual cold outside. Rubber heels squeaked busily on the polished floor and a fair-haired nurse bustled past. Stevie eyed her appreciatively. Nice pair of ankles in those black stockings, he thought, and even in the antiseptic nurse's uniform there was an exciting rounding when she bent over the old man in the bed in the far corner of the ward.

Here, I'm not so bad, he thought. Thinking like that showed he was almost back to normal.

He glanced at Joe, sitting morosely in the chair beside the bed.

"Cheer up, Joe," he said. "It might have been worse."

"It couldna be worse," said Joe viciously. "That bloody polis with all his questions. He didna believe us, Stevie, you ken that."

"Does it matter?"

"Of course it matters, ye gowk! He's going to report to

the procurator fiscal and we're going to be up in court."

"Eh? What's the charge?"

"No us. We'll be on the other side for wance. Witnesses. D'ye no see? Yon bastard shot ye. Ye've been brought in here and had the stuff taken oot of ye. That canna be kept quiet. So now they'll have the man on a charge of attempted murder or something."

"Attempted murder? Here, there's quite a stretch for that, isn't there?"

"Aye. Of course. Mebbe ten years. That wouldna worry me. I'd like fine to see the bastard put away for what he did to ye, but it's what'll come oot in the court besides."

"Like what?"

"Like I've been inside. Like there's been trouble before. Like mebbe if that comes oot the jury'll believe yon bastard fired in self defence."

"I don't see—"

"They might believe that we were poaching, see?"

"Oh."

"And it might get us the jyle. It wouldna be too bad for you, being the first time, but for me?"

"Hoo long might ye get, Joe?"

"I've no idea. Long enough."

They fell silent for a while. The man in the next bed seemed sound asleep, lying on his back with his mouth wide open, snoring loudly. He'd done that all last night, and what with the noise and the pain in his leg, Stevie hadn't got much sleep. But in spite of the man and the noise he was making they kept their voices low, not wanting to be overheard.

"Can ye no stoap it?" asked Stevie.

"What, the case? Stevie, wance the law gets moving ye canna stoap nothing. It just goes on and on."

Stevie wriggled thoughtfully, trying to find a position of ease for his leg.

"I kent we shouldna have tried it, Joe," he said.

"Tried what?

"The poaching. We dinna ken nothing aboot it."

"Paddie O'Donoghue tellt me all aboot it."

"Well, he didna tell ye enough. I never seen a fish in that pool at all."

"I ken. I dinna understand that. Yon Brian Blair tellt me

the Darroch was a grand river for the salmon. If we could have gotten even a half dozen fish, we'd have made a bit of siller off of yon auld wife at the big hoose."

"I wish ye'd forget aboot the auld wife, Joe. It hasna done ye much good so far."

"I canna forget the auld bitch. Arrogant cow. I'll get even with the swine if it's the last thing I do."

Vaguely Stevie thought that was an awful lot of animals to be contained in one person, but what really worried him was the viciousness in his brother's voice. Joe had got his knife into the lady laird and nothing would give him greater pleasure than to twist it really painfully. He knew in a perverted way Joe blamed the lady laird for their recent failure and for the injury which had been done to him. Joe's thinking was apt to take that sort of twist. He was never to blame for failure himself.

"Maybe the fiscal'll no go ahead with the case," he said hopefully.

Joe looked at him with some contempt.

"Ach, grow up, Stevie. These legal bastards, they'll make work for themselves every time they can. You ever met a poor lawyer? No. Well, that's why. Wance they get their teeth into something they'll never stoap till there's no more money to be made oot of it."

Stevie felt like saying that there wasn't all that much difference between the lawyers and their cases and Joe and the lady laird, but wisely he held his tongue.

Joe stood up.

"I'll need to go, Stevie. Get back to work. Okay?"

"Aye, Joe. I'll be fine. They're letting me oot tomorrow, so I'm no worried. See me, hirpling aroond with a stick, eh?"

"I'd like to see yon bastard that shot ye hirpling aroond with two sticks," said Joe, and went on to describe various other things he would like to do to him, none of which seemed remotely possible anatomically.

"Joe . . . "

"Aye?"

"I'm no keen on going into a court."

"Neither am I."

"Is there no way we can get oot of it?"

"No. If we try it'd just be suspicious. Look at it their

way, Stevie. If ye've been shot and ye ken who's done it,
the thing ye most want is to see the bloke who's done it
standing trial for it and getting put away for a bloody long
time, right?"

"Right."

"And that's how you feel, right?"

"Well—"

"'Course you do."

"No exactly, Joe. Ye see, we shouldna have been there.
Maybe the bloke was right—"

"Right to take a pot shot at ye? Ye're blethering, man!
Never mind whether ye should have been there or no.
You just think it oot, Stevie. Ye canna let folk go roond
shooting at folk because they're no in the right place.
That'd be anarchy, Stevie."

"I thought that was what ye wanted, Joe."

"What—anarchy?"

"Aye."

"Well, maybe ye're right. But it's *my* anarchy I want. No
theirs."

He punched Stevie gently on the shoulder and headed
for the door. Stevie watched him go and then sighed and
settled back against the propped-up pillows. There was
no point in thinking ahead to any kind of a trial for the
moment. Besides, after all that had happened he was
feeling a wee bit tired. Maybe it would all blow over . . .

5

Jimmy sat at the table in the window of the Auchtarne Tea
Rooms and sipped at the cup of coffee in front of him.
Through the window he could see the jetty where the
ferry boat was tied up, rocking gently in the light breeze.
Already one or two people had boarded her, ready for the
next trip to Glendarroch which was due—he looked at his
watch—in ten minutes' time.

The tea room was almost empty. He wondered how it
managed to keep going during the winter months when
there were no tourists around. In the summer it did a
roaring trade in ice cream and fish and chips and Coca
Cola, but now there was an inevitable air of neglect about

it. Apart from old Mrs Mitchell, the owner, sitting behind the counter reading the *Daily Record*, the tea room was empty.

There was also, so far as he was concerned, an air of loneliness. It was here during the summer that he had spent many happy hours with Marion Cochrane, Lorna's daughter, who was now at dough school in Glasgow and was not due to return to Glendarroch for a week or two. Looking back through rose-coloured glasses, those were the days, days which never seemed to end, the trips back and forth across the loch, with Marion growing more and more proficient in handling the boat and the mooring lines, so much so that words weren't necessary. She knew what had to be done without anything being spoken. There were times, he realised, when they had passed an entire journey without saying a word to each other, yet the ease and companionship had been complete. Funny how he didn't remember it ever raining during those days. It must have done, of course, but he had not been aware of it. Neither, he was sure, had she.

It wasn't that they had been in here that often. Only when it was raining. So it *must* have rained sometimes, he thought with a wry smile. Otherwise they would sit in the sun at the end of the jetty, eating their sandwiches, drinking coffee from the thermos, chatting of things which were immensely important yet didn't matter in the least.

He wondered what she was doing just now. Probably up to her elbows in a flour bowl, and undoubtedly there'd be a smudge of flour on the tip of her nose . . .

He grinned to himself and finished his coffee. Time to think about moving.

The door opened and Ken Calder came in. Jimmy looked at him in surprise.

"Hallo, Ken, what are you doing here?" he asked.

Ken grinned and went to the counter where he ordered a bowl of broth and a roll from old Mrs Mitchell.

"Back at Duff's Garage for a week," he called across. "Geordie Simpson's got flu so they're short-handed."

"You mean you've left my father slaving away over the peat cutting all by himself?"

"Yes. Do him good. He was beginning to get fat again."

Ken brought his bowl of soup and the roll over to the

table and sat down beside him.

"Heard the news?" asked Ken.

"About Dougal shooting the poachers? How could I have missed it?"

"Two of the blokes from Laird's Point, I hear," said Ken. He took a spoonful of soup and smacked his lips appreciatively. "I'll say this for Mrs Mitchell. She makes soup the spoon'll stand up in."

"Yes. Talking of which—"

"The soup?"

"No. Laird's Point—"

Jimmy nodded towards the window and Ken turned to follow his look. Joe MacMorran was turning on to the jetty and approaching the ferry.

"That one of them?" asked Ken.

"Yes. He'll have been visiting the one that got shot. His brother, I think."

Ken surveyed the man speculatively.

"I wouldn't like to meet him alone on a dark night," he observed.

"No. Neither would I."

"You had trouble with them?"

"No. None at all. There are six of them and they keep themselves very much to themselves. It's difficult enough to get a good morning out of them. That one in particular. The younger one's all right. The one that copped it from Dougal."

"D'you think they were poaching?"

"Of course they were poaching. What else would they be doing at Peddie's Pool at half past one in the morning?"

"But the fish—"

"I know there are no fish in the river. But they didn't know. They're from Glasgow. They probably don't know anything about the salmon cycle. How could they? But that was what they were after."

"Maybe you'd better go and tell the fiscal that," said Ken.

"Why?"

"Because Dougal's going to be charged."

"And go to prison?"

Ken scraped the last spoonful of broth out of the bowl

and then wiped the bowl with the last of the roll and put it in his mouth.

"It looks like it, Jimmy. It looks very like it indeed," he said.

6

The sun had gone from the windows of the ward and outside the day had become grey and threatening. Stevie awoke slowly and, seeing the view from the windows, wondered briefly where he was. The stertorous breathing from the bed next door reminded him. He had slept little the previous night, what with that and Joe's hare-brained expedition and then the discomfort of the wound in his legs, and after Joe had gone he had willingly given way to the waves of lassitude which swept over him.

He looked round and there was a face looking down at him. He blinked his vision clear and the face came into focus. For a moment he thought it was one of the nurses, but there was no cap surmounting the fair hair and although the features were familiar he didn't connect them with the hospital.

"Hallo," said the face.

"Hallo too," he said.

"I brought you these."

These were a bunch of grapes and he grinned broadly.

"Very conventional," said the face. "I'm sorry."

"Don't be. I'm glad to see them. And you. Have a seat."

He recognised her now. It was the girl who'd been with the lady laird at Laird's Point yesterday morning.

She sat down in the chair which Joe had occupied earlier and looked at him. There was something about her face which he couldn't identify, which he found strange. It seemed—empty was the word which sprang to mind. It had been empty yesterday and it was still empty today. But it was a nice face, one which Stevie appreciated.

"You're Stevie MacMorran, aren't you?" she said.

He nodded.

"Guilty," he said. "And who are you?"

"I'm Fiona."

That was the name the lady laird had called her by.

He'd forgotten.

"Hi, Fiona."

"Hi."

"Have a grape."

"They're for you."

"I couldn't eat them all. Help me."

"All right."

She took one and popped it into her mouth. It was a pity there wasn't more animation about her, he thought. If there had been more life in that face she would really be a very good-looker indeed. As it was there was—just nothing.

She picked the grape pips out of her mouth and flicked them into the disposable bag on his bedside cabinet. Somehow this action made her seem a little more human.

"I'm sorry about your accident," she said.

"So am I."

"But you shouldn't have been there, really."

She didn't say it accusingly or regretfully or angrily. It was just a statement of fact so he couldn't get indignant about it.

"We thought it was a short cut—" he began, repeating the story which he and Joe had agreed on.

She nodded as though that were unimportant.

"How long are they going to keep you here?" she asked.

"I'm getting out tomorrow."

"Oh, I'm glad," she said and it was as though she really meant it. For the first time there had been some life in her, and it seemed to change her whole personality. Well, not change it, but actually to give her some personality which she hadn't had before. He looked at her with a deeper interest.

"Is it very painful?" she asked.

"No, no really. They've patched me up pretty well. I expect I'll be able to play the violin again."

"Do you play the violin?"

"No."

"Then—"

"It's just a way of saying I'm okay. Anyway, I wouldn't play the violin with my feet."

She looked at him uncomprehendingly for a moment and then suddenly a smile came to her face and it was as though the sun had appeared from behind a cloud.

"Oh, I see. Sorry. I didn't understand—"

"Have another grape," he said.

"No. You'll need them. The food here must be terrible."

"No, it's fine."

"Really?"

"Great. Tomato soup, roast beef and peaches and ice cream for lunch."

"Gosh, that's better than I got . . ."

"Got when?"

She looked down at her hands.

"When I was in hospital," she said.

"You've been in hospital?"

Suddenly the sun went in again.

"Yes," she said, and stood up. "I must go. Can I come and see you again?"

"Of course. Any time. But make it soon. I'll be oot tomorrow."

"What time?"

"I dinna ken. They havena tellt me yet."

"All right," she said. "I'll be here. Goodbye."

Stevie watched her go, chewing thoughtfully on a grape. What a very odd conversation. And what a very odd person. But nice. And quite a stunner too. There was something pretty titillating about being visited by a member of the aristocracy. Wait till he told Joe . . .

No. Perhaps he wouldn't. Joe wouldn't approve at all. And somehow this was something Stevie wanted to keep completely to himself.

7

The tractor had been coughing like an asthmatic yowe and Dougal had spent a good half hour tinkering with the engine, trying to find the cause of the trouble. He would really have to have a word with Ken Calder and see if he could come up with a magic solution of some kind, for there was no doubt the problem was beyond him, though he didn't want to admit it. Because to do so meant he would have to stop working on the tractor, acknowledging that all this dirty pointless labour was just a way of passing the time. He needed something to do and yet he didn't want to be far away from the house.

Damn it, why didn't they come and get it over with?

He straightened up as he heard what he had been half-dreading all morning—the sound of a car engine approaching the croft house. He was almost sure he knew what that would mean. And at long last the waiting was over.

He stepped out of the barn and looked up to the track and there it was, sure enough, the white Ford Cortina with the bright red stripes of the Strathclyde Police and the blue light on top, travelling slowly and carefully on the uneven surface.

Dougal's heart sank. In a way he had had the feeling that it had all been a dream, that nothing further would happen, but if that were so, then it was evident that he was about to be rudely awakened.

The car stopped in the yard and Sergeant Murray got out. He stretched himself, nodded solemnly to Dougal and waited while the constable driver switched off and got out as well.

"We'd better go inside, Dougal," said Murray.

Wordlessly Dougal nodded and led the way into the house. Grace had heard the car and had almost automatically gone to put the kettle on. She turned from the cooker with the kettle in her hand as Dougal led the way in, and the constable and Sergeant Murray followed. Dougal glanced at his mother and quickly looked away again. He didn't like to see the distress in her face.

"Good morning, Sergeant," she said.

"Mrs Lachlan."

"Sit down. And you, son," she said to the constable standing just behind him. The constable made a slight move towards a chair but was stopped by a glance from Murray.

"You'll have a cup of tea," said Grace, but her voice said that she already knew that the offer would be refused.

"I won't, thanks Mrs Lachlan. This is an official visit, I'm afraid," said Murray.

He stood at the fireplace, his hands behind his back, looking very solemn and Dougal's heart sank still further.

"You'd better sit down, Mother," he said with uncharacteristic concern for the state of his mother's health.

There was something in his voice which made Grace for once in her life obey him immediately and, putting down the kettle, she sat quietly at the table.

Murray tugged his notebook out of his pocket.

"I have been instructed by the procurator fiscal to charge you formally with assault with a dangerous weapon," he said and Dougal blinked at him.

"A dangerous weaon? A shotgun at seventy or eighty yards?"

"Assault with a dangerous weapon," said Murray.

Dougal felt his legs weak and he sat down beside his mother at the table. Murray was going on, something about being bound over to appear in court when the case was called and that if he wanted to say anything it would be taken down and maybe used in evidence . . .

"It's a lot of nonsense," he said, and Grace laid a hand on his arm as Murray began to write in his notebook.

"Don't say anything, Dougal," she said anxiously. "Isn't that right, Sergeant? It would be better if he said nothing at all."

"That would be better, Mrs Lachlan," said Murray sympathetically.

"You'll need to get a lawyer," said Grace, her hand still on his arm, and when he glanced at her he saw that there were tears in her eyes. Funny that that should make his own eyes feel suddenly hot and red. He blinked rapidly.

"Aye. Well, maybe I'd better," he muttered. "But it's daft, I tell you . . ."

"Dougal, you shot the man," said Grace. "With a shotgun. You assaulted him with a deadly weapon. There isn't any doubt, is there?"

Dougal looked from her to Murray and to the constable who was staring into the middle distance as though his mind were far away.

"No. No, I suppose not," he said. "But I'll fight it. I'll fight it all the way."

"Aye, you will," said Grace. "You certainly will. And I'll tell you this. You'll have the whole of Glendarroch behind you."

She looked up defiantly at Murray who swallowed and put away his notebook. He nodded, glanced surreptitiously at the constable, and nodded again.

"Aye, that's right, Mrs Lachlan," he said. "But if you take my advice, Dougal, it's a lawyer you'll be needing behind you now."

Chapter Three

1

Joe shivered. The pew was hard and uncomfortable and the church was obviously only heated for the Sunday service. It was very cold. Not the most pleasant place to spend a March day.

He'd had a look round. Bare sort of place. Some nice wood. But the ornaments and flower vases weren't worth a penny. In fact there wasn't anything worth flogging anywhere.

He thumbed through a Bible he'd found on the ledge in front of him. What a lot of words, he thought. Words and poverty. That was what it amounted to, this religion business. It wasn't for him. The opiate of the people, Marx had called it, and by God he was right. If things weren't going your way there wasn't much point in falling on your knees and begging for help. You had to do your own thing.

And that was what he was here for, of course. But he wished she'd get a move on. He was getting corns on his tail sitting here, wasting time.

The door at the back of the church opened and hastily he composed himself in the pew, sitting back and adopting an attitude of soulful prayer, hands over his eyes, and waited.

"What are you doing in here?" demanded a female voice.

He looked up mildly and smiled.

"Good morning, madam," he said turning off his Glasgow accent and turning on the charm. "I was sitting here meditating."

"This is no place for meditation."

She really was an old battle-axe, he thought. Brian had been right when he had described the village gossip-monger. With that face like a sour jeely piece, a shapeless old coat and an upturned chanty on her head, there was no doubt that this was the celebrated Mrs Mack.

"Oh, I'm sorry," he said humbly. "I do beg your pardon. Is it inconvenient if I sit here?"

The tone of his voice and the respect in his demeanour seemed to crack the granite exterior to some extent.

"I have my work to do," she said with slightly less severity. "Thursday is the day I clean out the church."

And she rattled the bucket she carried in her hand as though to prove the point.

That was what Brian had said. So far his information had been remarkably accurate, though he still didn't understand what had happened to all the fish Brian had said were in the river Darroch. Unfortunately the day he had spoken to him at the back of the shop he hadn't quite got all the information he wanted and now, after that abortive raid on the river he couldn't very well go and question him again. Brian would doubtless have some suspicions that the attack on the river had been a result of what he had told Joe, and he doubted if Brian would have been taken in by the story of having missed their short cut home. So he couldn't go back and dig more information out of him under the guise of friendship. But Brian had spoken at length about Mrs Mack and looking at her, he thought that providing he could win her confidence she would prove just as reliable a source and probably provide even more information.

"I have no wish to disturb you," he said. "I simply— well—I do like to spend what spare time I have in church. . . ."

He left the sentence hanging and she rose to the bait as he had hoped she would.

"Why?"

He looked down at the ground as though embarrassed by the question.

"I had hoped at one time to—to enter the ministry," he said, putting as much regret into his voice as he could.

She looked at him with a little more interest than she had shown up till now.

"Why didn't you, then?"

He smiled sadly.

"Circumstances," he said. "I began my studies at St Andrews University."

"Divinity?"

"Divinity. Alas, it could not last."

"Why not?"

"My father died. There was no money. And I had to return to look after my ailing mother and my little brother and my two helpless sisters."

He wondered if he hadn't gone a bit too far, but she was properly hooked.

"I see," she said with grudging approval. "That was a most charitable action."

"It was the least I could do. I did my best, but there . . ."

He let the words trail away.

"What happened?"

"My mother died. In my arms. And she made me promise to look after my brothers and sisters. Of course, I did so. I would have done so even without the promise. You know."

"I know," she said, though she didn't look as if she'd ever looked after anyone out of the goodness of her heart in her whole miserable life.

"And I have done so ever since. Though it has not been easy. Hard labour is my lot, madam. Not for me the ministering to the sick and the frightened, bringing comfort to the dying and relief to the troubled. But hard toil with only the strength of muscle God has given me. I have already had some satisfaction in seeing my brother placed in a job, and with God's help I shall endure until each of my sisters is set in some rewarding rôle in life or received into the bosom of a worthy man who will love and cherish her."

He could go on like this for hours, but he thought he had probably given her enough now.

"You're at Laird's Point," she said, her eyes suddenly widening with realisation. "A workman," she added in disapproving tone.

He bowed his head in acknowledgement.

"Are you one of those Dougal Lachlan shot at?"

Damn it, she was too wide awake. He had hoped she wouldn't make the connexion.

"Innocently strolling in the still of the night communing with nature, madam, and we were set upon—"

She clicked her tongue with impatience.

"He should be taught a lesson," she said.

He breathed an inward sigh of relief. She was on his side after all.

"Oh, charity, charity," he said. "No, no. I am sure he acted for the best. Though it is surprising how misguided our best can often be, is it not so? Alas, it was my brother who was injured through no fault of his own. I wish it had been me and that he could have gone unharmed."

"Your feelings do you credit," said Mrs Mack. "How is your brother?"

"He is, I am glad to say, out of danger and should not be detained for long in hospital. I came here to pray for him and for his quick recovery. Like me he needs his physical strength to earn an honest crust of bread."

"And I'm glad you're taking Dougal Lachlan to court," said Mrs Mack.

He shook his head.

"It is not we who are taking him to court. Had it been left to us I should have said, let him go. Go, I would have said, and sin no more. But the law takes its own course, and nothing we can say will stop it."

Mrs Mack sniffed. It was a telling sniff and echoed round the high rafters of the church.

"But we must not speak of such unpleasant things, and I must not keep you from your work. But tell me—" he went on hastily as Mrs Mack showed an inclination to terminate the conversation and move away, which was the last thing he wanted at the moment. "This is a most beautiful part of the world."

"On the surface, perhaps. It is very different underneath."

"Quite beautiful. But what do you find to do here? How are the people gainfully employed?"

"There are very few who are gainfully employed. Most of them are lazy and idle and never come to church either."

"Dear me. But there must be activities of some kind . . .?"

He let the question hang and she picked it up as a spider pounces on a fly. He listened as she laid off about the iniquities of the lady laird—a subject on which their views seemed remarkably close—about the way in which she ground the faces of her tenants into the dirt, and how some of them were attempting to wrest a living from the earth, and Joe listened to everything she said, rejecting the references to people's personalities but picking out the items which interested him. According to Mrs Mack about ninety nine per cent of the people in the village were either lazy or immoral or uncivilised or a combination of any of the three, and not one had a redeeming feature. The remaining one per cent seemed to be herself and her late husband who, despite having had a great many strange turns of phrase to enliven the dead hours of existence with this woman, must have died almost with relief.

Eventually she ran out of steam and Joe said that he had enjoyed their stimulating conversation, asked her if he might return to the church for further meditation, permission was graciously granted, and he left her to her bucket and mop and went out of the church into the cold grey light of the outside world.

Once there he grinned to himself. What a ghastly old bat, he thought. But useful. Very useful indeed. And she had given him the information he wanted.

2

Elizabeth looked at Dougal. He was being stubborn, of course, which was no more than she would have expected, but under the stubbornness was an uncertainty, perhaps a fear, which was foreign to his nature. Dougal could often be wrong, but never in his own mind.

Yet now he was wondering.

She felt responsible for what had happened. After all, to some extent Dougal had been acting in defence of her property. And now that she knew that one of the men involved in the poaching incident had been the one who had been so uncivil to her at Laird's Point she was quite prepared to believe that their intentions had been to lift salmon from the Darroch. She rather regretted that it was the younger one who had got injured. She scarcely remembered him, her attention having been on the other, but she seemed to think that what impression she had had of him had not been unfavourable. By comparison, anyway, but then that was not saying very much.

She drew her attention back to George Carradine who

was sitting opposite Dougal, also at the other side of the desk.

'It seems to boil down to this," said George. "You thought he had a gun and you fired in self-defence. You don't deny having fired at him with intent to prevent him from committing an assault on your person."

"That's right, Mr Carradine," said Dougal.

"So the only defence we have to offer the court, to my mind, is that you genuinely thought he was going to fire at you."

"I did," said Dougal.

Carradine sighed.

"Yes," he said. "But the point is that the man didn't carry a gun. Neither of them carried a gun. Unless, in that split second before you fired and Bob Taylor appeared, they managed to fling it away or secrete it somewhere where it hasn't yet been found."

"There's no point in going on about the gun, Mr Carradine," said Dougal firmly. "There isn't a gun. The police have searched the area. Bob and I have searched the area. There is no gun. And I know now that I made a mistake. He didn't have a gun. Because I watched him after I'd fired and he didn't try to throw anything away. And when he spun round I saw that his hand was empty."

Carradine sighed again and shook his head.

"Honesty is a great thing, Dougal, but where a court of law is concerned it is possible, perhaps, to be too honest. You will do your case no good if you admit all this in court quite so openly as you have here."

"Why shouldn't I? It's the truth I'm telling."

"Yes, I know, but—"

"And I understand that it would be necessary in a court to tell the truth, the whole truth and nothing but the truth, isn't that right?"

"Indeed it is, but there are ways of doing it . . . Never mind."

George Carradine brushed the subject away with a wave of his hand. Elizabeth could sympathise with him. Testimony such as Dougal's delivered in the way Dougal delivered it, if reproduced in the witness box could damage his case beyond redemption.

"I'm not quite sure what kind of defence would be

possible," said George. "We might dwell on the criminal character of the older brother. He has been in prison and is known to the Glasgow police for a variety of offences ranging from demanding money with menaces to impersonation. But unfortunately the pursuer in this case is not Joseph MacMorran but Stephen MacMorran, and there is nothing known about him."

"They are brothers, though," said Elizabeth.

"Indeed, and one might perhaps highlight the effects of association and the natural influence which an older brother may have, and there is no doubt that the two were together when the event took place. But it's all confoundedly thin."

"Would it not be possible to break down their story?" Elizabeth asked. "I mean, the idea of the two of them being out for a quiet, innocent stroll up by Peddie's Pool at two o'clock in the morning is quite ridiculous."

"It certainly is," said George. "And I'm quite sure it will cause a few smiles in the jury box. It would be easy to cast ridicule on it, but unless you can prove that it didn't actually happen that way, you're really no further forward as far as the law is concerned. You must remember that there is no law of trespass in Scotland, unless you can prove that wilful damage was being caused. I'm sure that will be Counsel's opinion."

Counsel . . . The word seemed to drop into the conversation and spread outwards like the ripples caused when a stone is flung into a pool of water. Like Peddie's Pool, thought Elizabeth, remembering how as a child she had lain on the bank there throwing pebbles in and watching the ripples spread to the bank while her father fumed and waited for the sun to go in so that there would be some point in trying a cast . . .

"Counsel," she said.

"Yes. I shall have to brief Counsel."

"You can't handle the case yourself, George?"

"The charge is too grave for a Sheriff Court, Elizabeth. This a High Court matter. You need a top advocate. And I doubt whether he can do much. I'm sorry, Dougal, if I sound pessimistic. That's because I am pessimistic. Mrs Cunningham knows you acted for the best and I'm convinced of it too. But convincing a court of law is a very different matter. I know the fiscal's office in Auchtarne. Paterson's a clever man and he has several very able deputes. To them the case will be very clear cut."

"Is there nothing we can do?" asked Elizabeth.

"Find evidence," said George. "Evidence that they were actually engaged in poaching. Any kind of hard, factual evidence."

"Or make them confess," said Dougal.

George eyed him sternly.

"If you're thinking of trying threats, Dougal, that would be extremely unwise," he said.

"I'm not thinking of threats, Mr Carradine. I'm just trying to think of *anything*. And to tell you the truth I'm not getting very far."

"No. I don't think any of us is," said George. "These men, according to you and Bob Taylor, set off an explosion."

"They did."

"Now where was this?"

"Peddie's Pool."

"Are you sure of that?"

"No. I'm not sure of anything. But that's where they were and they were waiting for the fish to come to the surface. So that's the most likely place for them to try it."

"I know it's the most likely place for them to try it if they're experienced poachers, Dougal, but we already know that they're not, or they wouldn't have been trying to mine a river at this time of year. So what guarantee have you that they would try to set off an explosion in the very pool they were looking in? Isn't it possible that they might have thought that setting off the explosion in a higher pool might have brought the fish down to Peddie's Pool?"

Dougal frowned.

"It's a daft enough way of thinking to be what they would have thought," he said.

"So it's quite possible that the explosion took place at some distance from Peddie's Pool."

Dougal sighed.

"Aye. Aye, I suppose that could be right," he said glumly. "And if it is it means we've got a much bigger area to think about."

"Exactly," said George. "Don't look so glum, Dougal. It

gives you hope, don't you see? You've searched the immediate area of Peddie's Pool and so have the police. And nobody has found anything. So, assuming that an explosion took place—"

"It did," said Dougal indignantly.

"Yes, yes, I'm being legalistic, I'm afraid. It's a habit I have. Assuming an explosion did take place, it rather looks as though it might not have taken place actually at Peddie's Pool. Perhaps we should widen our area of search."

Dougal grunted and looked unconvinced.

"It's worth thinking about, Dougal," said Elizabeth.

"Aye, aye, Mrs Cunningham. It is that. And I'm grateful for the wee bit of hope. But it's a muckle great area and even in March there's enough cover to hide a battleship in. And aren't we forgetting one thing?"

"What's that?" asked George.

"They might not have left any evidence behind."

"Oh, surely. You can't set off an explosion without leaving something behind, can you? I mean, I'm no expert," said George as though anyone might have thought he was, "but there must be—what—detonators? Fuses? Wire? Batteries? I don't know, but something. And they had nothing on them when they were found and there is nothing in the area where you found them. So where is it?"

"Och, there is no knowing what they were thinking at all," said Dougal gloomily.

"A new search will have to be made and the police will have to supervise it."

"I can't see Sergeant Murray being thrilled by that idea," said Elizabeth.

"It will have to be done. We must leave no stone unturned. Trite, but true."

"Or blade of grass either," said Dougal despondently.

"Indeed. It must be done. It may be your only chance, Dougal," said George.

3

There was a thin drizzle of rain and it wasn't nearly so

cold as it had been, yet Stevie shivered as they left the
warmth of the cottage hospital.

"Lean on me," said Fiona, and he did so, partly because
suddenly facing the outside world again like this made
him feel a bit shoogly on his legs, and partly because he
enjoyed the physical contact. He grasped the stick firmly
in his right hand and put his left on Fiona's shoulder.

"All right?" she asked.

"Fine. Just give me a second. Okay. Let's go."

He began to hobble across the car park towards the
road beyond. There was a flower bed bordering the road
full of dead roses, their withered leaves and some of last
year's blooms hanging sadly towards the ground. To begin
with his right leg felt as though the skin were being
stretched tight across the bone, but as the activity continued the feeling eased away and by the time they
reached the road he felt he no longer needed Fiona's
support. He continued to take it, though.

"Where are we going?" he asked.

"The Auchtarne Tea Rooms," she said. "I'm going to
buy you a cup."

He grinned at her and they headed down the road
towards the jetty.

He glanced sideways at her face as they went. It had
changed since he had first seen it two days before, become
more responsive. There was life there now and it stirred a
new excitement in him.

He scarcely noticed the drizzle of rain as it soaked his
hair and began to drip down the back of his collar. Fiona
wore a headscarf with horses' heads on it, and he pictured
her in riding breeches, mounted, hair flowing free under
her riding cap, at the gallop . . . Great . . .

The tea room was empty and the jetty which they could
see from the window contained no boats. The loch beyond
was a steely grey fading into mist towards the opposite
side so that you couldn't see the mountains beyond
Glendarroch at all. Stevie sank with relief into a chair
while Fiona went to the counter and was greeted like a
long-lost daughter by the old biddy behind it. A minute
later she brought a tray with two cups and a plate
containing two pieces of Mrs Mitchell's home-baked
shortbread. He felt in his pocket.

"How much was that?" he asked.

"Nothing," she said.

"No, I'm paying."

"You're not. It's my treat."

"First grapes. Now tea. Is there no end to your generosity?"

"Perhaps not."

He grinned at her and she smiled back across the table. Wow . . . That smile did things to you . . .

The tea was fresh and hot and the shortbread was delicious and they sat in a companionable silence for a long time. Occasionally a figure shrouded in gleaming oilskins or huddled under an umbrella hurried past on the wet pavement outside, but here they were isolated in a little cocoon of warmth.

"Do you really want to take Dougal to court?" asked Fiona suddenly, and he blinked at the unexpected directness of her question.

"Dougal? Is that the bloke who potted me?"

She nodded.

"Dougal Lachlan," she said.

"No really. I suppose we shouldna have been there. Private property and all that . . ." he said, mindful of Joe's injunction to say nothing about their real purpose.

"He thought you had a gun," she said as though she were excusing him.

"I ken. But I hadna. I dinna take a gun on a country walk as a rule."

She stirred a finger through the shortbread crumbs on the plate as though intent on what she was doing.

"Couldn't you stop the case?" she asked.

"Joe says no. Now it's started it's got to go on."

"Does he want it to go on?"

"I'm no sure. It's no easy to ken what Joe's thinking. To begin with he was dead against it. Didna want to say anything to the polis nor nothing. But now. I'm no so sure . . ."

He stared unseeingly out of the window down at the deserted jetty for a while.

"Couldn't you get him to stop it?" she asked.

"Like I said, no one can stoap it noo. And noo I dinna think Joe wants to stoap it. I think—"

He stopped himself. He was about to say he thought that Joe was now enjoying playing the part of the injured party, brutally assaulted in the middle of an innocent walk. He might have gone on to say that Joe was basically motivated by wanting to see both Dougal and the lady laird grovelling in the dirt, and a court of law would be the best place possible for them to do it in. But he didn't. After all, this was the lady laird's daughter . . .

"What do you think?" she prompted him.

"I think you're a very bonnie lassie and I think I'm beginning to like ye far too much."

She laughed and he got the feeling that was something she hadn't done for a long time. There was something—unpractised about it.

"Don't change the subject," she said.

"Why no? It's a much nicer subject to talk aboot. Tell me aboot yourself."

A shadow crossed her face briefly.

"There's nothing to tell," she said.

"There must be. Living in yon big hoose. What aboot all the cocktail parties and the coming oot balls and the hunting, shooting and fishing boy friends?"

She frowned.

"You don't know anything about it. There's nothing like that. I may live in a castle but we have to pay rates on it."

He felt he'd put his foot in it somehow, that she had withdrawn from him a little, and he wasn't quite sure why.

"No boy friends?" he asked, because that was a question which suddenly seemed rather important.

That blank look crossed her face again.

"No," she said shortly.

Stevie had a certain amount of sensitivity, and he knew he had trodden on dangerous ground. She'd been hurt. By a man. Sometime fairly recently, and as the thought came into his head he felt a wave of sympathy for her flood through him. It all fell into place. That pale, blank, empty face he had first seen. The gradual thaw in the hospital. The animation in the tea room and the withdrawal when boy friends were mentioned . . . Then there had been her reference yesterday to being in hospital. What kind of a hospital had it been. . . ?"

Suddenly he saw her not just as a pretty girl with a rich

mother living the sort of life which he knew nothing about, full of parties and hunt balls and trips to the Riviera whenever life got too boring here, but as a small hurt creature, a bit helpless, very vulnerable, someone in urgent need of protection . . .

He swallowed. It was a rare moment of awareness and it brought with it a touch of fear. He wasn't the person to help her. Not him. Not Stevie MacMorran from Easterhouse whose brother had been in jail and who spent his days labouring at a demolition job, on the lump because he couldn't get proper work . . .

Perhaps he should get up and go. Say thanks for the tea and the shortbread, it's been nice knowing you, Fiona, orrabest, cheerio.

But he couldn't do it. She needed him. Well, he thought honestly to himself, not *him*. But she needed someone, and in the absence of anyone better he supposed he'd have to do.

Something to say. The silence was stretching too far. What could he say that wasn't going to hurt her. . . ?

"I'll lend you my brother if you like."

He waited for her reaction which was a long time in coming. She seemed to return from a vast distance and hear what he said a long time after he had said it. She smiled suddenly and he breathed a quiet sigh of relief.

"You sound as if you're frightened of him," she said.

He considered the question seriously.

"I suppose I am in a way," he said. "He's no wan to cross, is Joe. A real tough guy. Much tougher than me. He's a tearaway, Joe."

"You *are* frightened of him."

"Dinna get me wrong. He's been good to me, Joe has. A real good brother. I've got a lot to thank Joe for. I dinna ken where I'd be if it wasna for him."

"Were you poaching?"

The question nearly knocked him off balance, it came so suddenly and unexpectedly. Damn Joe and his crazy ideas. . . !

"Poaching?" he echoed. "Who'd go poaching at this time of the year?"

She looked at him searchingly.

"No, indeed," she said. "Who would?"

Because Stevie knew now from what had been said since the shooting incident that Joe had blown it. There weren't any damned fish in the river so the whole business could have been avoided. And maybe Joe felt guilty that Stevie was the one to suffer from his mistake, and because of that someone else would have to suffer instead . . .

"Thanks for the tea," he said.

She smiled as they stood up.

"That's all right. Can I walk you home?"

"If you dinna mind me leaning on you again."

She looked at him very directly.

"I don't mind," she said. "In fact, I think I quite like it."

"Good. 'Cause I quite like it too."

He picked up his stick and they headed for the door.

Outside the drizzle still fell and the world was quiet, blanketed by the rain and the mist. They turned, heading in the direction of the digs which he shared with Joe— where was Joe, by the way?—and he put an arm round her waist.

She looked down at it expressionlessly.

"That won't give you much support," she said.

He grinned.

"No. But it may give some to you," he said.

She looked at him a little warily, then nodded as though she agreed with him, and they set off along the road.

4

It had been worrying Isabel all afternoon and when she heard the back door open and the clunk of Brian's boots as he shook his feet out of them before coming in, she hurried through to the kitchen.

Brian stood in his stocking soles, closing the kitchen door, the boots in his hand. He was very wet but cheerful.

"What a day. It's like glue up there," he said. He took off his glistening anorak and hung it over the back of a chair before going to the sink to wash his hands.

"Brian—"

"Aye?"

"Mrs Mack was in this morning."

Edith Macarthur as the 'Lady Laird' Elizabeth Cunningham.

On the way back from church are Brian and Isabel Blair (played by Kenneth Watson and Eileen McCallum), the owners of the Glendarroch Store.

One of the best known characters on the Glendarroch Estate, Dougal Lachlan the crofter (played by Alec Monteath), and his constant companion Tav.

Men with an important part to play in the running of the Glendarroch Estate—Archie Menzies the Estate handyman (played by Paul Kermack) and Bob Taylor the gamekeeper and water bailiff (played by Iain Agnew). Despite the problems (above) they still manage to have an amicable disagreement! And of an evening they can enjoy a game of 'summer-ice' (below), a table-top version of curling, which is a popular winter sport in Scotland.

Bill Henderson as Ken Calder and Joan Alcorn as Lorna Seton pose for the camera during a break in filming outside the 'big house'.

Young Kevin Shearer, known to millions of Take the High Road *viewers as Wee Donald, tries to get Floor Manager Morag Torbet (right) interested in the art of blowing bubbles. As for Muriel Romanes, who plays the part of Alice Taylor, Kevin is apparently unimpressed with her bubbling talents!*

"Anything unusual about that?"

"No. It was what she said—"

"Again?"

"She met that man. Joe MacMorran."

"Don't tell me there are wedding bells. That would be just the thing for Mrs Mack."

"Brian, she met him in the church."

Brian turned, his hands dripping, forgetting to pick up the towel, and stared at her in astonishment.

"What was he doing there?" he asked. "Pinching the plate?"

"Mrs Mack said that he was meditating."

"Joe was doing what?"

"Meditating."

Brian frowned, found the towel and began to dry his hands slowly and thoughtfully.

"Did he say that or did she?"

"He told her that was what he was doing."

Brian stood stock still for a moment, then flung the towel over the rail again and headed for the living room.

"I don't like that very much, Isabel," he said.

"I didn't like it much myself. But you know what she's like. Full of praises after that. What a kind and thoughtful man. If there were more like him here Glendarroch would be a better place. All that sort of thing."

"I can imagine. What made her say all these nice things about him?"

"He told her he was a divinity student at St Andrews and had had to give up because his father died and he had to go home and look after his ailing mother and a large family—"

"What a load of blethers! Joe MacMorran was born in Easterhouse in Glasgow and I don't think he ever got further than primary school. He probably got chucked out of that too. What on earth did he tell her all that rubbish for?"

"To impress her?"

Brian stared at her and his face became very serious.

"Aye. To impress her. And why? To get information out of her."

"I wondered. But what sort of information would he be after?"

"Information about the village. What goes on here. Who's got silver hidden away in the press. And he couldn't have gone to a better source . . . God!"

He stopped suddenly and slapped his forehead.

"What is it?"

"It's my fault. When he came here a few days ago he started asking me about the place, what there was to do here, how I made out, all the rest of it. I didn't say too much because I know Joe. But I did mention the Darroch and what a good river it was for salmon and that we got a lot of fishermen here in summer . . . That's why he went for the Darroch, God help me. It was my fault . . . I never thought . . ."

"But there was no harm done."

"Except Dougal's been charged with assault with a deadly weapon and is going to have to stand trial."

"*That's* not your fault—"

"I'm not so sure of that. Anyway, it's not the point. I told him about our celebrated gossip, Mrs Mack, the fount of all wisdom. It was a joke thing, really. I told him she was the minister's housekeeper and she cleaned out the church and the village hall and that was how she kept up with the gossip . . . I think I even said that she cleaned the church on a Thursday . . ."

"And he went there deliberately to get information from her."

"Exactly. And posed as a poor failed divinity student who had put his humanity before his prospects. Just the sort of thing to impress Mrs Mack."

"But why?"

"Because he failed at the Darroch, that's why. Joe doesn't like failure. And his brother copped it because of him. Of course, to Joe that wasn't Joe's fault. It was Dougal's. Now he's going to get revenge on Dougal, and probably Mrs Cunningham too."

"Why Mrs Cunningham?"

"Because she's Mrs Cunningham. Landed gentry. Landed gentry are the dregs in Joe's eyes. They should be abolished. He'd have been a dab hand helping with the French Revolution."

"You really think he'll try again?"

"Yes. Yes, I do. The question is, what? And when? And

where?"

"There's only one person can answer that. Mrs Mack."

Brian looked dubious.

"Aye. I daresay. But to her Joe MacMorran is the blue-eyed boy at the moment. And you know her. Nothing we can say will make her change her mind."

"You'll have to try."

Brian nodded gloomily.

"Yes. I'm afraid I will," he said.

5

The drizzle was still coming down as though it never meant to stop. There was the sound of rushing water as the burns filled and chuckled more and more rapidly down their courses and the bare branches of the trees dripped large drops into the undergrowth. It was as though the whole earth had come alive too early in the year.

The old bat had been talkative. And she had been accurate.

Joe MacMorran climbed the track from the road until it petered out for no apparent reason. It continued as an ill-defined path meandering between bushes of elder and bramble but running roughly parallel with the road a quarter of a mile away and a hundred feet lower, still climbing as it went.

He paused for breath. This sort of heavy activity was not his usual way of life and he didn't take kindly to it. But the rain was a help, although it was uncomfortable, for it meant that there were probably no prying eyes watching him. It was getting late, the evening was setting in early, and he would have to do what he wanted to do fairly quickly if he was to find his way back to the road before it got too dark to see where he was going. He wouldn't fancy being caught out here in this weather all night. If the rain stopped and the sky cleared it might get very cold indeed.

After ten minutes hard walking up a very steep slope he found his way blocked by a fence. Wide mesh and about seven feet high. He moved a little way to his left and found a padlocked gate. He rattled the padlock but it was large and effective and the gate itself was very firm.

He began to follow the wire to the right. It wasn't easy. The path had expired at the gate and now in places the undergrowth came right up to the wire and he had to force his way through soaking bushes which tore at his legs, impeding progress. But he was so wet that it didn't seem to matter very much.

He paused and brushed the hair out of his eyes, feeling himself sweating profusely from the exertion, but in spite of that there was a savage satisfaction in him, warming him to a trembling eagerness.

After about a quarter of a mile he came to another gate, also padlocked, also very firm, and here he found a track which led away from it. Unlike the previous gate this one seemed to be a main entrance and vehicles must sometimes come up here, though they would have to have four-wheel drive to negotiate the steepness and the sharp turns and the rough conditions.

Joe took a last look at the fence and began to follow the new track down the slope. Water was running down the twin grooves where wheels had worn away the surface. In the fading light it looked grey, sometimes black. It wasn't used often, he noticed, for the branches of trees and bushes projected over the track and none seemed to have been snapped off. The track twisted and turned its way in hairpins down the slope and he followed it while the evening gathered in around him and he tried to hurry without going too fast and risking a fall, perhaps spraining an ankle. That wouldn't do at all . . .

Ten minutes later and in very murky light he came to a gate in a small wire fence which led into a fairly large clearing with a floor of flattened boulders and stones. He tested the gate. It was held only by a drawbolt, but it was hinged at the far side with bits of orange twine so it sagged a bit as he opened it. No problem, though. He closed it behind him and cast around in the clearing, searching for the continuation of the path downwards.

This must be a turning point for heavy vehicles, for he found the further track down without any problem. It was very much wider, obviously more frequently used and despite the weather the surface was quite drivable for a large vehicle.

Joe nodded approvingly as he made his way down this track which descended at a much shallower angle and without the hairpin bends of the higher one.

Another ten minutes brought him to a further, bigger gate, also closed but not locked, and beyond it was the road.

He tried the gate. It had proper hinges and opened easily once he had unhitched the chain which bound it to the gatepost, and he replaced it carefully once he had passed through.

He found himself standing in an indentation in the road, a sort of natural lay-by and he looked up and down in the last of the light. He had timed it pretty well. There was still no one around and he recognised the section of road he was standing on. It was about a mile from Glendarroch which lay to the right, and about eight from Auchtarne which lay to the left.

That was fine. The first track he had taken had only been a hundred yards or so from the first houses in Glendarroch, and was far too close for comfort. This one was ideal.

Joe shrugged deeper into his anorak, thrust his hands into its pockets and, uncaring about the weather, began to walk towards Auchtarne. Eight miles was a long way, and the night was not the best for walking, but with any luck someone would pass in a car and offer him a lift.

He rather hoped it might be the lady laird . . .

6

Isabel switched off the television set as Brian came into the living room.

"Well?" she asked.

Brian sank into his chair with a sigh of relief. It had been a long day and dealing with Mrs Mack at the end of it had added considerably to its length.

"I don't know," he said.

"Didn't you ask her?"

"Oh, aye, I asked her. At least I brought the chat round to it, because if I'd asked her direct she'd have clammed up. She was awful busy. Far too busy to speak. You know

her way. Down on her hunkers, washing the hall floor as
though the girl guides had contaminated it."

"It was the scouts this evening," said Isabel automatically.

"Well, whatever. I just asked her about Joe MacMorran.
He's made some impression on her, I can tell you. If only
there were more like him round here this place would be
safer and healthier. All that rubbish."

"Did you find out what she'd told Joe?"

"She's told him everything, from what I can gather.
Who's married to who, who's living with who, who's
children are whose. And what everyone does and what
everyone's worth. Though in Mrs Mack's eyes I don't
suppose *that'll* be much."

Isabel stared thoughtfully at the blank television screen
as though seeking information from it.

"I even risked asking her what he seemed most interested
in. Everything, she said. Obviously his great humanity and
care for people made him interested in everything they
did or said. She really must have gone her dinger with
him."

"Oh, Brian . . ."

He sat back with a sigh and put his hands behind his
head.

"Well, there's one thing we can be thankful for," he said.

"What's that?"

"There's only one of them now. If the younger one's
been injured he'll not be very mobile for a while, so Joe'll
be on his own. Maybe he won't be able to plan anything,
and from what I hear, the work at Laird's Point won't last
all that long. Ken Calder had a word with one of the lads
in Henderson and Speirs's yard yesterday and he said he
thought it would be a fairly quick job."

"So maybe he'll be away before he can do any more
damage."

"Maybe. We'll just have to wait and see."

7

The first train out of Auchtarne should leave at seven
minutes past seven in the morning, but it rarely did. It was

a well-known local saying that if it started on time from one end of the platform it would be late by the time it reached the other, and that Saturday morning seemed no exception.

It eventually rumbled into the station at half past and Joe MacMorran climbed thankfully aboard. The waiting room had been shut and the door was locked and he didn't want to draw attention to himself by kicking up a row at the ticket office and demanding the key, so he had stood for over half an hour on the open platform, the chilly dawn wind seeking out gaps in his protective clothing, while the daylight brightened blearily. He had read all the advertisements telling him how cheaply he could get to London, though they failed to say how long it might take. There was an old poster, tattered and torn by the winter gales, on which he could still see a family of four, a child of each sex aged about seven and nine and a bronzed and happy father with his arm round a shapely bikinied mother, neither of whom could have been over the age of 25, disporting themselves on a beach at Skegness. It all seemed slightly out of place and totally unbelievable on that windy, deserted platform frequently swept by scuds of sleety rain.

No one else seemed to be joining the train this morning. On a Saturday in summer the platform would have been thronged with tourists with their rucksacks and their camping gear, but even during the week in the winter few people used the train. It was too unreliable, too slow and too inconvenient. The internal combustion engine had taken over.

A flurry of rain blattered against the carriage window as the train began to pull out, and from the safety behind it Joe watched the loch appear on the right hand side of the line and slide past faster and faster as the train gathered speed until the rising ground of a cutting obliterated the view.

Two and half hours later, and by now three quarters of an hour late, the train drew to a halt at Queen Street Station in Glasgow, and Joe got out with about a hundred other passengers who had gradually joined the train as it ambled through the glens and into the sprawling mass of the city, stopping at almost every lamp post to pick people up.

The rain had set in now and he stood at the bus stop just off George Square, shrugged deeper into the anorak, wondering why rain always seemed more soaking and more annoying in a city than it did in the country.

The bus itself smelt of damp and the windows were covered in condensation so that he had to wipe a hole in one of them to see out. Not that there was much to see. Old grey tenements gave place to high rise blocks, and then to a wilderness of uninspiring council houses, each with a small square of garden, most of which had run to seed long ago as even those who had tried to take a pride in them had given up the unequal struggle against human vandalism and the depredations of stray cats and dogs. The gutters were choked with plastic containers, broken bottles and empty beer cans. Joe felt a sense of familiarity and comfort. This wasn't Glendarroch. This was home.

He got off the bus and walked along one narrow seedy street after another where the lamp standards were broken and many of the windows were the same. There didn't seem to be anyone around. It was just about as deserted as Glendarroch. The rain, which had strengthened into a persistent downpour, had successfully driven everyone off the streets.

He stopped outside a house where a broken wooden railing had once kept the grass and flower beds safe, but had long ago given up trying. There were still flakes of a cheerful blue paint here and there on the broken staves, but they were few and far between. The lower floor of the house at the top of the broken concrete path had boarded-up windows where someone, or many people, had been busy with different coloured paint sprays, advertising the names of rival gangs or of individuals seeking some sort of release from anonymity. Joe remembered doing this sort of thing himself not all that long ago. But he had other things to think of now.

He went into the close mouth and climbed the stair to the first floor. There was an old dustbin lying on its side on the landing and the place reeked of tom cats and stale fish and chips.

There was no name on the peeling paint of the right hand door and after trying the bell a couple of times he realised it didn't work, so he knocked and waited.

After a moment the door opened a fraction on the end of a chain and a face looked out at him. The face needed a shave and the hair needed a wash and the nose needed a blow, but Joe recognised it.

"Hullo, Prettyboy," he said.

"Just a minute," said the face and the door closed. Joe heard the chain being removed and then the door was fully opened and the face was revealed to be attached to a body clothed in a black leather jacket with metal studs, faded denims with patches on each knee and heavy boots with, Joe knew though he couldn't see them, fairly substantial tackets in them.

"You got something, Joe?" said the face.

"Got it in wan, Prettyboy. Got it in wan. Aye."

"Come in then, fella. Come away in."

Prettyboy stood aside and Joe went into the house.

The door closed behind him.

Chapter Four

1

There hadn't been a word spoken for about a quarter of an hour, and soon it would be time to part. His arm was round Fiona's waist, but it wasn't there as an excuse for support now. He no longer needed the stick. The leg was healing nicely and he could walk without any suspicion of a limp, although he couldn't go very fast or very far. But his arm seemed to be where it was by mutual consent. At least she had never wriggled free or asked him to keep his hands to himself.

The evening had cleared miraculously after rain all day, and now the sky was steely blue, fading to grey as the evening gathered. The wind had dropped with the clearing sky, but the waves on the loch had not yet gone down and were still battering themselves angrily on the shingle just where they walked.

There was something he had to say and he didn't know how to say it. He felt it might cause her pain, she who had become so much more natural and animated over the past four days. So instead he broke the long silence by asking something different.

"Why did you come to see me in the hospital?" he asked.

She was silent for so long he wondered if she had actually heard the question or whether she was off again in one of those strange withdrawals which still afflicted her now and then.

"I wanted to," she said at last.

"Why?"

"I don't know. When I saw you that first time. With Mummy. At Laird's Point, remember?"

He nodded. "Mummy" seemed so terribly upper crust that it was almost alien to him, yet coming from her it seemed quite natural, so he didn't smile at all.

"I remember," he said.

"I just liked you. I didn't like your brother."

"I was a wee bit struck on you myself."

"Were you?"

"Oh, aye. No doubt aboot it."

"Good."

He squeezed her waist and for a moment she laid her head against his shoulder. Almost by mutual consent they stopped and stood looking out over the loch. They were beyond Auchtarne here, away from the houses which bordered the loch. In the summer there would be families picnicking here, children running in and out of the water, and their parents dozing in the shade of the trees which hung their branches out across the shingle. Now there were no people apart from themselves and the trees were just skeletons weaving a tracery in the sky above them.

He sensed that she was nervous for some reason. There was a tension in her body which was not the same as that total blankness he had been aware of before. He felt her tremble.

"Stevie," she said.

"Mphm?"

"Would you mind very much kissing me?"

He turned her gently to him and looked into her eyes. They were worried, frightened by something but not, he thought, by him. She has been ill-used, he thought. Someone has done something terrible to her.

"I wouldna mind at all," he said.

"Gently, please."

He took her face between his hands and drew her to him. Her lips were dry and irresponsive. He heeded her request and simply brushed them lightly with his own.

He broke away and looked at her.

Her eyes were closed and she seemed to be savouring something. He said nothing, but waited. After a while she nodded and opened her eyes again.

"Thank you," she said softly.

"All right?"

"All right. Yes. I'm fine."

He'd actually meant did I do it right, but she'd taken it another way, perhaps he thought, telling him that she'd survived or hadn't found it too distasteful.

"Thank you," she said.

They turned back to look out over the loch, and there was another silence. Anyone recording this would have a pretty blank tape, he thought.

"Someone hurt you," he said at last, which was what he had wanted to say earlier.

Again she didn't reply and he wondered if perhaps he had gone too far, opened a wound which was trying to heal, but she didn't withdraw from his encircling arm and after a while she nodded.

"Yes," she whispered.

"Do you want to talk about it?"

An emphatic shake of the head.

"No," she said.

"Fair enough."

"I'm sorry. I don't."

"That's all right."

"It wasn't his fault."

Funny that she said she didn't want to talk about it, because she began to do so. Slowly at first and then faster and faster. Soon it was all pouring out of her in a crazy jumble of words, so disjointed that he found it difficult to follow, but he gathered that there had been a farmer and there had been an affair which had been doomed from the start, and that her mother had been against it and her mother had been right, and that she had found him one day with someone else and she'd had an accident and no one knew whether it was an accident or whether she'd tried to commit suicide and she wasn't sure herself, and that was why she had gone to hospital, not an ordinary hospital but a mental place, and the hurt which she had sustained had been a grievous one but it had been at least half of her own making.

She said it all standing at the loch side looking out over the water, never at him, and somehow he felt he was standing aside, like one of those priests with someone confessing, that she was purging herself of guilt and pain, and that was all right by him.

There were tears, too. She didn't sob, but when he stole a look at her face turned blindly towards the loch, he could see them pouring unheeded down her cheeks.

The words stumbled to a halt at last. He turned her to him and wiped the tears off her cheeks with his thumbs.

"Better now?" he asked.

She nodded and fished in her pocket for a handkerchief and blew her nose very loudly and inelegantly, not at all what should be done at the hunt ball.

"Yes. Thank you. Thank you for listening."

"May I kiss you again?"

She thought rather seriously about that for a moment and then nodded very definitely.

"Yes," she said. "Oh, yes, please."

And she put her arms round his neck and drew him to her, moulding her body to his and this was a very different kiss from the last one and he felt his heart beginning to pound, not so much with excitement as with a heavy and inevitable regret.

2

"We'll need to stoap for petterol," said Scruffy.

Prettyboy swore. In the four days since Joe had come to see him he'd performed miracles of organisation. Mind you, with his connexions that wasn't too difficult, but nevertheless he felt he'd done the job of a leading general in a major war planning a vital campaign. Was it all to be thrown away now?

"Did ye no fill it before we started?" he demanded.

"Aye, I did, Prettyboy," said Scruffy a little shrilly, his eyes switching rapidly from the road to the fuel guage and then to Prettyboy beside him in the front passenger seat. "Honest I did. I filled it. Right to the brim. Poored oot, it did, it was that full."

"Billy said this land-rover would do thirty to the gallon," said Prettyboy.

"Well, it's no doing it, Prettyboy. Nowhere near it. More like seventeen, I'd say," said Scruffy.

In one of the back seats Dracula grunted.

"What do ye expect from Billy Richardson? He's a car salesman. They never tell the truth," he said.

Prettyboy thought furiously. He'd thought the land-rover would have got them to their destination and at least most of the way back before they'd have to call at a filling station, and by the time they did they'd be far enough away not to excite attention.

"You'll need to find a garridge," he said.

"Aye," said Scruffy with another anxious glance at the

petrol guage. "And gey soon too."

There was silence as the land-rover roared and rattled its way along the road. It wasn't the newest of land-rovers. In fact it was in a fair way to qualifying as one of the oldest. But Billy Richardson had assured him it was good for a few thousand miles yet, and Billy Richardson should know better than to try to pull the wool over Prettyboy's eyes. If it all went wrong because of Billy Richardson Prettyboy would get The Progger to execute a new design on his face.

The Progger was sitting beside Dracula at the back, his blank eyes staring without interest at the passing scenery. The Progger was not one to say much. In fact The Progger hardly ever said anything, but if you were organising this sort of expedition he was the man you wanted to have with you. The Progger, as his name suggested, was at his best with the knife, but he was at home with a sub-machine gun too, though from his face you could tell that he didn't think it was capable of the artistry of a knife.

"There's no many petterol pumps oot here, is there?" said Dracula as though the fact had just dawned on him. "What happens if we run oot?"

"Then you walk to the nearest wan and get the lend of a jerrycan," said Prettyboy.

"Where's that?"

"Probably ten miles ahead."

"Here, I'm no walking that far," Dracula protested.

"If we run oot someone'll have to," said Prettyboy.

"Could we no turn back?" asked Dracula, having considered the problem at some length.

Prettyboy sighed. Dracula was a useful person to have on a trip like this for his sheer physical strength, but there were times when his lack of mental strength made you want to boke.

"Hoo far since the last garridge, Scruffy?" he asked.

"Aboot twenty-five miles," said Scruffy, and silence descended again.

"There's no many petterol pumps," Dracula observed as though all this proved the point he'd been trying to make in the first place.

It had been so carefully organised. Maybe too carefully, thought Prettyboy. If he hadn't had to think of so many big things he might have thought to sling a couple of jerrycans full of petrol in the back of the land-rover, though if what Scruffy said was true, that they were only averaging something like seventeen to the gallon, it wouldn't have made all that much difference. But at least they wouldn't have been caught short so close to their destination.

Organising the land-rover had been bad enough, but organising the refrigerated van had been something else. It was surprising how many contacts he'd had to go through to reach Eric Lumsden who drove a refrigerated van for a wholesale butchers in the Gallowgate and who thought it might have been possible to sort of borrow it for a night. Negotiations had taken a long time. Eric must have known that there was some urgency in Prettyboy's request, although he'd tried not to let it show, because he'd hummed and hawed and put off until he'd squeezed a much higher cut out of Prettyboy than Prettyboy had envisaged at first. However, a bargain had been finally struck and now, all being well, that refrigerated van would be following them a couple of hours behind. He hoped that it, at least, wouldn't run short of fuel.

It was all in the timing, really, and he thought with some relief and satisfaction that having to stop for petrol wouldn't make any difference to that. But there was more chance of the van being remembered at a filling station than simply passing innocently through along with dozens of other vehicles. He didn't like the idea of having to stop.

"Where's this?" he asked.

"Auchtarne," said Scruffy as they passed the nameplate at the town limit.

"There'll be a garridge here," said Prettyboy.

"Thank Goad," said Dracula. "I'm needing a pee."

"You're no getting oot for a pee," said Prettyboy. "Ye'll bide in the back there and keep bloody quiet, d'ye hear me? If ye really need a pee ye can wait till we get where we're going."

"I doubt I'll no can wait that long," said Dracula.

"I doubt ye'll have to," said Prettyboy firmly, and Dracula subsided.

Scruffy slowed down to a sedate thirty as they passed the limit posts. Prettyboy nodded approvingly. One thing about Scruffy was that you could rely on him to carry out orders to the letter. Scruffy loved driving. He loved driving very fast and Scruffy was good. You got quite a kick driving with Scruffy at the wheel. There was nothing he liked more than cornering on two wheels or spouting up gravel in folks' faces from a fast take off, but Prettyboy had said right at the beginning that this trip they mustn't break the law, mustn't give the polis any reason for stopping them. After all, all four of them had records, and all four being found in one car might be just a wee thing suspicious.

They neared the centre of the town, passed the school, closed for the day now, then a bingo hall which had once been a cinema. The public library. No garage.

"There's got to be wan somewhere," muttered Prettyboy.

He glanced down at the fuel guage. The needle was hovering ominously on empty. The last thing he wanted was to run out and have to push this damned contraption to a garage to fill it up. They were supposed to be keeping what was called a low profile. If they had to do something like that they might as well have brought a pipe band with them.

"Hey!" said Dracula suddenly.

"What?"

"There's a Shell sign."

"Where? Where?"

"Just ahead there, see?"

"So there is. Thank Goad for that. Right. Drive in, Scruffy, and leave the rest to me."

"Okay, Prettyboy, you're the boss," said Scruffy, and he turned into the forecourt of Duff's Garage.

3

Their lips parted slowly and he looked down at the top of her head. At first she wouldn't look up at him and then reluctantly she raised her head and met his eyes, and he saw there a mirror of his own regret.

It gave him the courage to say what he had wanted to say for some time now.

"It'll no do, will it?" he said softly.

After a moment she shook her head in agreement.

"I'm sorry," he said. "Maybe we didna ought to have started—"

She shook her head again, but this time it was in negation.

"No," she said. "I'm glad we did. It—helped."

He took hold of her and pressed her to him again, but there was now no passion in the embrace, merely a form of protection which he knew he would have to relinquish.

"There's too much difference," he said. "Our worlds are too different. You ken things I dinna ken. Mebbe I ken things you dinna ken. In fact, I do. And the most of them's things you wouldna want to ken anyway . . . No. It's better no to let it go too far, eh?"

"I know," she said. "This is what they call a rebound situation, isn't it? That's what I'm on. A rebound. And it's not a good enough reason for forming a relationship."

"Just remember this. I'm no on the rebound. And I was as smitten as you."

She smiled at him a little tremulously.

"Was?" she asked.

He grinned.

"Well—all right. Still am, I suppose. But I'm no the wan to put you on my white charger and ride off with you into the sunset. Where would I take you? The digs here in Auchtarne? I doubt if you'd like them. The hoose in Easterhouse? I canna see ye settling in there. It's no exactly your scene. And I'm no coming to live in yon castle, I can tell ye."

She nodded her agreement this time.

"I know," she said. "I just wish—"

She broke off and bit her lip.

"Wish what?"

"I wish I'd met you first, that's all. I think it would all have been kinder and happier and—and maybe easier to end."

He squeezed her gently and then released his hold on her.

"Better be going," he said. "The ferry'll be away in ten minutes and if ye miss it ye may have to spend the night in the digs after all."

D.I.T.G.—E

They began to walk along the shore of the loch. He felt for and found her hand and held it. It was small and smooth in his and seemed to him to symbolise the difference between them. His was big and muscular, hardened and calloused, the fingernails torn with dirt under them. Hers was delicate and unused to manual work. And that was true of the two of them in general.

And yet there was a tenderness in him for her, too, and he would do a great deal to help her. Thinking of what might happen soon he wondered if there wasn't something he might do to help her more, but it really meant helping her mother rather than her and he wasn't sure whether he wanted to do that.

They passed the first houses standing above their gardens at the edge of the loch and by mutual agreement the physical contact ended. Here was another symptom. She was known here as the daughter of one of the local gentry. It wouldn't do if she were seen holding hands on the lochside with one of the labourers at Laird's Point.

The sands were running out. He should have gone back to Glasgow a couple of days ago. Joe had told him to, that he couldn't expect to work at Laird's Point with his injured leg and the job would be over by the end of the week anyway. But he had refused up until now. And he realised that he had refused because he had wanted to go on seeing her.

Which was stupid. It wouldn't work. It couldn't work. And what was more it shouldn't work. He would be doing her no service spinning out a relationship which was doomed from the start.

He had determined to break it off tonight, finally and irrevocably and when she had told him about her hurt he knew it was even more important that he should do so, that she should not become so emotionally involved that it might all happen again.

Tomorrow he would take the train back to Glasgow and he wouldn't ever come back to Glendarroch or Auchtarne.

The jetty came in view round a curve of the shore and he could see the ferry boat tied up at it. There didn't seem to be anyone in sight and he stopped, making up his mind to say what he had to say before they got any closer to prying eyes.

"I'll no see ye again," he said.

"Won't you?"

"Well, I'll no be around Glendarroch any more. There's nothing I can do at Laird's Point now with this." He slapped his leg. "And I dinna think it would be sensible."

"No. It wouldn't be."

"So we'd better say cheerio here."

She blinked a little and nodded.

"Yes," she said. "All right."

"But just before we do there's something I ought to say to ye."

She looked a little scared for a moment and then realised that whatever it was it wasn't going to be a suggestion of any kind of physical involvement as a parting gesture.

"Be careful of Joe," he said. That was it. It was out now and he couldn't withdraw it. In a way he felt disloyal to the older brother he had always loved and sometimes supported, but during the last few days his loyalties had become curiously divided, partly through this girl in front of him and partly through Joe's hotheadedness which had brought him his injury. And also because of what he feared Joe might be up to now.

He hadn't seen much of Joe recently. Stevie, of course, had not been at the site, but he'd heard from the others in the gang that Joe had been frequently absent, setting them tasks and swearing violently if they were not finished in the allotted time. And on the occasions when he had been on site he had driven himself hard to bring the job to an early conclusion. Stevie's only personal knowledge of all this was last Saturday when Joe had gone off to Glasgow early and had not returned until very late at night. Stevie had wondered what had taken him so far for such a short time, but when he'd asked, Joe had told him to mind his own business. It had nothing to do with him . . .

So there was something afoot, he was sure. He had no idea what, but he was pretty certain that whatever it was it would be another attempt to get even with the lady laird, and probably with the bloke with the shot gun, the two present focuses of all the frustration and hatred which festered away in him all the time.

"Why?" she asked. "Why should I be careful of your

brother?"

"I dinna ken. And maybe that's why I'm telling ye. If I did ken I might no tell. But watch him. He's got his knife into ye."

"Into me?"

"Well, no you particularly. Your mother mainly. And that bloke that shot me. And he's plotting something. Though I dinna ken what it is."

She frowned more in puzzlement than anger.

"Why would he want to do that?" she asked.

"You dinna ken Joe. I do. It's the sort of thing he'd do. I just want ye to be careful, see?"

She still looked puzzled, but she nodded.

"There," he said. "That's my wee parting present. All right?"

He put a hand under her chin and raised her face to his. He kissed her gently, almost paternally and he felt her lips respond briefly. Then he let her go, looked at her once more and turned and walked away up the shingle to the path which led down between two houses towards the loch side from the road.

When he got there he looked back and saw her still standing where he had left her. He raised a hand and then turned away when she didn't respond.

Two minutes later when he reached the road and looked back at the shore between the houses he saw she had turned and was walking slowly along the shingle towards the jetty and the ferry which would take her back to Glendarroch.

4

Ken Calder came out of the office as the land-rover drew into the forecourt.

It stopped between the nearest pumps and the office itself and when he came round the tail of the land-rover he found that one of the passengers had stepped out and was looking in puzzlement at the pump.

"It's okay," he said. "I'll do it."

"Can I no do it myself?" asked the man with the growth of beard and the dark greasy hair.

"It's not self-service," said Ken. "Sorry. We're converting next month. Till then you get personal service. How many?"

"Fill her up. She'll maybe take ten."

"Right."

Ken unscrewed the petrol cap and inserted the hose pipe and began to fill. The man stood beside him, fidgetting uneasily.

"Not a bad day," said Ken conversationally.

"No."

"We could do with a decent spell after the battering these last few days. But it's going to get colder."

The man grunted.

Not a great conversationalist, thought Ken. As the petrol poured into the tank—which from the sound of it must have been nearly empty—he glanced idly at the land-rover. Pretty ancient and a Glasgow registration.

"Oil all right? Need any water? Tyres checked?"

"No."

"Okay."

Conversation languished again and the fidgetting went on. Through the window Ken could see the driver sitting hunched over the wheel and in the driving mirror he caught the shadowy shapes of two people sitting in the back, but with the hood up he couldn't see much more. And yet . . .

He felt prickles down his spine. Some primitive instinct was warning him. What was it?

Whistling gently he moved so that he could get a clearer view in the driving mirror. One of the two men in the back came into sharper focus. He was carrying something. A canvas package, long and thin like a trumpet, maybe. But the man didn't look like a musician.

The pump stopped and the petrol lapped the edge of the filler. Ken returned the hose to the pump, his heart beginning to beat a little faster. He read off the figures.

"That's sixteen pounds fifty-two, please," he said.

The man peeled notes off a wad he produced from his pocket, two fives and seven ones, and handed them to Ken.

"Keep the change," he muttered.

"Thanks."

The man opened the passenger door to climb back into the land-rover and as he did so Ken got a much clearer view of the occupants before the door closed again.

The engine started and there was a squeal of tyres as the land-rover made a clumsy racing start and slewed out of the forecourt on to the road which fortunately happened to be empty at the time.

Ken hurried after it as it disappeared and stood on the pavement watching it.

At the junction at the end it didn't turn right to continue on the main road northwards, but took the minor road to the left. Towards Glendarroch. Glendarroch and nowhere else . . .

Ken stood thoughtfully for a moment and then hurried back to the office. He rang the money into the till, pocketed the change—no point in missing out on that, he thought—and then picked up the telephone. Quickly he dialled Glendarroch House. With any luck Lorna wouldn't have left yet. The silence in the receiver was broken by a long continuous buzz. Unobtainable . . .

He frowned and tried dialling the number again. The same thing happened.

Next time he dialled the Glendarroch Store. Brian probably wouldn't be home yet but Isabel would take a message and pass it on . . .

The same continuous buzz . . .

He slammed the receiver down, urgency rising in him now, and then picked it up again and dialled 100.

This time he heard the normal double ring and he sighed with relief. It went on for a long time while he leant on the counter drumming his fingers on it impatiently.

"Operator, can I help you?"

"I'm trying to dial a Glendarroch number," he said. "Getting the unobtainable signal—"

"There is a fault in the line to Glendarroch. We are doing our best to rectify it and hope to have normal service restored shortly."

Ken swore under his breath.

"How short is shortly?" he asked.

"I am afraid I have no further information."

"Thanks a bucketful," he said and put down the

receiver. Suddenly this had become very serious.

Then a thought struck him and he glanced at the clock on the wall. There might still be time . . .

He left the office and sprinted for the repair shop at the back of the garage.

"Charlie—keep an eye on the forecourt will you?" he shouted to a pair of dungareed legs which poked out from under a jacked up Ford truck. "Back in a minute."

There was an answering shout of acknowledgement from under the truck and Ken turned and raced out of the forecourt, glancing anxiously at his watch as he did so.

5

"You should come back to the Aqua Sports," said Jimmy. "The new season'll be beginning soon and help will be urgently needed."

"Won't Marion be back?" asked Fiona.

"Yes, but only in the holidays. She'll be here for Easter which is a mercy, but then there's a long time before she gets off for the summer. I'll be slaving away on my own. Eddie'll help, of course, but I need someone reliable."

"To do the typing."

"That too."

"I might . . ."

He looked at her as she sat on the thwart, wondering what had happened to her. She seemed to have woken up again, which was a relief, and he wondered what had caused the awakening. But there was a sadness in her too. Still, at least that was a copper-bottomed emotion, something which she hadn't shown any sign of for long enough. He supposed it was a step in the right direction.

He glanced at his watch. Almost time to go, but being the last ferry he usually left a few minutes late in case of stragglers, but there was no sign of any tonight. It looked as if he and Fiona were going to be the only two on the crossing.

"Jimmy!"

The voice came from the head of the jetty and looking up he saw Ken standing there, looking a little breathless.

"Hi, Ken," he called. "You coming over?"

"No. I've got the car. Just a word . . ."

"Mind the shop, will you, Fiona?" he asked as he scrambled on to the jetty and he saw her nod briefly as he stepped towards the road where Ken was standing. There had been something in his voice which made Jimmy hurry.

"Jimmy, I think there's trouble."

"What kind of trouble?"

"A land-rover with four men. One with a firearm of some kind. Could be a sub-machine gun. Heading for Glendarroch."

Jimmy stared.

"What do they think Glendarroch is? he asked. "The O.K. Corral?"

"I mean it, Jimmy. I recognise the types. Cheap hoodlums from Glasgow."

"What do you think they're after?"

"I know what they're after, but there's a fault in the telephone line and I can't get through. You've got to go back and warn the folk. The crofters particularly. Dougal. The Moncurs. Inverdarroch. The Stewarts and MacNeill. You've got to warn them."

"But who—?"

"They tried for the salmon and made a mess of it. Now they're going to have a shot at the deer farm. And when I say a shot, I mean a whole great lot of shots. It looks like they want to clean the place right out!"

6

There really was very little cover at this time of year, but using what there was Mr Murdoch edged forward between the trees until he had a good view of the clearing in front of him. He scanned it carefully.

Nothing.

He sighed. It looked as if he would have to return home empty handed.

He felt the weight of the rabbit in his left hand coat pocket and that was fine, but Mrs Mack had asked for something for the minister's lunch tomorrow, so there was so far nothing for himself. Mrs Mack, of course, took first place. It was as well to keep friendly with Mrs Mack. It wasn't easy to do so, but the consequences of doing anything else could complicate life considerably, seeing that he was the kirk session clerk and she was the minister's housekeeper.

He was getting to the stage where even the sight of a pheasant would have been welcome . . .

Of course, he told himself piously, it would have to be a cock bird, if anything. It was seven weeks past the end of pheasant shooting, but as there was no official shooting on the estate it didn't seem to him to matter too much whether the birds were allowed to breed or not.

As Mrs Mack might have said, the Lord helps those who help themselves, and Mr Murdoch was quite an adept at helping himself, certainly to things for the pot which might be found lying around here and there. But tonight unfortunately he hadn't been able to take her saying at face value. He'd helped her, but not himself. He discarded the idea of a pheasant. For one who didn't mind taking in unidentified packages at the back door, Mrs Mack had curious double standards on the subject. A rabbit is one thing, she would say, a pheasant out of season quite another. And no doubt she was right. He wouldn't have shot a pheasant even if he had found one.

Would he. . . ?

He refused to answer the question and turned his mind to trying to pick out another rabbit. Usually at this time in the evening they would have been out airing themselves, but of course the mild, rainy, blustery weather had gone, leaving clear skies and a rapidly dropping thermometer, so perhaps they were content to remain in the comfort and warmth of their underground burrows. He always found his mind picturing Beatrix Potter-like scenes of a mother rabbit in a starched apron stirring a pan full of vegetables while copper pots gleamed on the walls and the children frolicked around her, and then it became rather difficult to shoot the things when they appeared. Maybe the limp bundle in his pocket should at this very moment have been at home puffing contentedly at its pipe before the fire and catching up with *The Rabbit Times* . . .

Not that it looked as if his conscience was going to be further troubled in that way this evening.

He crossed the clearing, disturbing nothing as he went, and plunged into the trees on the further side. The next clearing would be his last for the light was beginning to fade now and he would simply have to go to the manse, deliver the one rabbit to Mrs Mack and go home and open a tin of corned beef for himself.

He pushed his way through the undergrowth, the shotgun cradled in his right arm, his deerstalker hat pulled well down as though by doing so he could hide himself from any inquisitive eyes. His foot caught on something in the undergrowth and he kicked clear of the obstruction, but it seemed to cling to him and he bent down to remove it.

It was a large plastic bag.

He tutted in irritation. Really, these tourists in the summer left so much rubbish behind them . . .

In the fading light he caught lettering printed on the bag and just before he threw it aside to continue polluting the area he made out the words.

Henderson and Speirs. Contractors. Auchtarne.

Something stirred in Mr Murdoch's mind and he paused with his arm drawn back in the act of throwing and then lowered it slowly.

Henderson and Speirs. That was where those two men worked. The ones Dougal Lachlan had shot at.

Mr Murdoch drew back his arm and again let it fall to his side without releasing the bag.

He had no great love for Dougal Lachlan. There had been bitter quarrels about the respective merits of their two dogs for one thing and Mr Murdoch still smarted at some of the insults which Dougal had hurled at him at that time. Of course, he had hurled a few in return himself, but still . . . On the other hand, Dougal was one of them, a member of the little self-contained community which made up Glendarroch. And like everyone else in the village Mr Murdoch was quite sure that Dougal hadn't taken a pot shot at the man without a very good reason. Whatever faults Dougal might have, letting off guns at people wasn't one of them. The story had been put about that the men were poaching, although there had been a certain amount of laughter at the idea of trying to mine salmon in March. Now there was a possible connexion.

The police had been looking for evidence. And this spot was only twenty yards from the river, though considerably lower down than Peddie's Pool where the incident had taken place.

Thoughtfully Mr Murdoch folded the plastic bag and pushed it into the capacious pocket of his overcoat, the one which didn't contain the livestock—or in this case the deadstock—tutting to himself as he did so. It crossed his mind that he was engaged in the same kind of pursuit that those men from Henderson and Speirs had been attempting, but then of course, he was local. He had a right to livestock from the open hillside in this area. They were incomers and had no such right. On these occasions Mr Murdoch tended to become a little confused over what was game and what was vermin.

He hunkered down and began to cast around the area where he had come into contact with the plastic bag.

After a minute or two his hand found something hard and square and smooth and he picked out a PP9 battery. Since it was quite clean and showed no sign of corrosion he assumed it had not been there for very long . . .

Mr Murdoch straightened up and glanced around slightly nervously. These were, as the saying goes, hot goods, he thought, and he had no wish to be found with them on his person so far from help.

But he knew what he was going to have to do.

He took a handkerchief out of his pocket and tied it to the bush under which he had found the goods. Then he had a last look round the area to impress it firmly on his mind so that later on he could come back with those concerned and point out the position to them. Many years of activity with the gun ensured that he knew this whole area like the back of his hand and he would have no difficulty in coming back.

Then, putting the battery in the same pocket as the plastic bag, he cradled the gun again and set off in something of a hurry, thoughts of potting another rabbit or even a pheasant quite driven out of his mind.

7

"But I don't understand, Fiona. How did you find this out?"

Elizabeth looked at her daughter in astonishment, not only because of the news she had just blurted out breathlessly as soon as she had entered the sitting room of the flat without even waiting to take her coat off, but also because of the change in her and the fact that she had actually volunteered some kind of information without having to be asked for it. And what information!

"Please don't ask me, Mummy," said Fiona, and Elizabeth made herself pause. She had to be careful. Too much pressure might make Fiona revert to the condition she had been in ever since she came back from the home, and the last thing she wanted was to undo whatever good work had been done with her to cause this change.

"Sit down, dear, and tell me calmly and slowly. You think that man MacMorran is planning something?"

"Yes."

"What is he planning?"

"I don't know."

"Fiona, this is all very well, and it wouldn't surprise me if he was planning to blow up the entire estate along with Laird's Point, but you must see that I can't do anything about it unless I know a little more. Please will you tell me what makes you say this? Perhaps we can work something out together."

The appeal for cooperation between the two of them seemed to work, for Fiona sat down on the edge of a chair and clasped her hands tightly on her lap.

"Stevie said so," she said quietly, so quietly that Elizabeth could scarcely hear her.

"Who is Stevie?" she asked.

"His brother."

"Joe MacMorran's brother?"

Fiona nodded, her head lowered, taking an inordinate interest in the intertwining action of her fingers.

Elizabeth drew in a deep breath and bit off an impatient retort. So that's where Fiona had been these last four or five days. Hob-nobbing with the brother of the man who had been so disgracefully rude at Laird's Point. She sat back in her chair and looked at her daughter wonderingly. First Geddes at the Home Farm, now this young labourer from Laird's Point. Elizabeth was no right-wing fascist, but really there were limits . . . Then she stopped to think. She began to recall the younger man at Laird's Point. She had paid little attention to him because all her thoughts had been on the string of rudeness coming from the other, but she recalled a quieter man, quite good-looking in a coarse sort of way, a man who had once or twice answered her questions when his brother refused to do so, quietly and without vulgarity, almost as though he were half-ashamed of his brother's attitude and behaviour. Yes, she mustn't judge them as being both of the same quality.

But what had gone on between this young man and Fiona that he had entrusted her with a confidence which involved the actions of his own brother? That was something Elizabeth didn't care to contemplate, and she knew better than to play the heavy Victorian mother and demand to know. Standards of behaviour had changed since her young day, she knew, and what would have been abominable conduct then was perfectly acceptable now.

And really, so long as Fiona hadn't been hurt again, that was what really mattered. And from all appearances she hadn't been. At least, not in the same way. And the old emptiness had gone . . .

There was, perhaps, a sadness about her now which tugged at Elizabeth's heart strings, but even that was better than nothing, and it was a gentle sadness, not a total despair such as must have brought about her previous emptiness because to allow any kind of emotion to enter her would have caused unbearable pain.

And gradually Elizabeth began to see things through Fiona's eyes, getting an inkling of what might have happened. She remembered the look on Fiona's face when she had first seen this young man at Laird's Point. Had that been when the first cracks in the veneer of emptiness had appeared? And had Fiona then pursued those cracks to open up the void and let human emotion in again? And now the predominating emotion was sadness . . .

"You've been seeing this young man," she said gently.

Fiona seemed to understand the tone of her mother's

voice.

"I took him grapes in the hospital."

"Did he enjoy them?"

"Yes. So did I."

"And you've seen him since."

"Yes. He helped. He was kind."

It sounded all so simple and perhaps it was.

"I'm glad," said Elizabeth.

"You needn't worry, Mummy. I shan't see him again."

"Fiona—"

"We decided. This evening. It wouldn't do. For either of us. He's catching the train back to Glasgow tomorrow and he won't come back. Not ever."

Elizabeth didn't quite know what to say.

"I think that's probably very wise," she said tentatively at last.

"Yes, it is. He said so too."

Perhaps this young man had a great deal more to him than his brother had, thought Elizabeth, beginning to feel a sense of gratitude towards him.

"And he said to watch out for his brother. That was his parting present, he said . . . Oh, Mummy. . . !"

And suddenly she was sprawled on the floor at her feet, her head in Elizabeth's lap and she was sobbing her heart out. Elizabeth stroked her hair gently, feeling the tears on her own face, tears of sympathy for this lonely girl she still thought of as being a child sometimes, and she sat there while the healing sobs went on and she said "There, there, it's all right" over and over with complete inadequacy till the sobs lessened and died away, and even as they did so she wondered what on earth she was going to do, not with Fiona, for that seemed reasonably straightforward now, but about the threat which she had brought with her that evening from Auchtarne.

8

Archie puffed along behind Mrs Cunningham in a state of total confusion. Well, not total, because at least he knew where they were going, but he certainly didn't know what for.

She'd come to the flat above the stables where he'd been just about to open a can of baked beans for his tea, and demanded that he follow her at once to Laird's Point. And to bring a torch, because it might be dark by the time they started back.

It had taken him a while to lay his hands on a torch and by the time he had done so she'd already started, striding out across the garden towards the gate at the foot, and he'd had to run to catch up with her. Whatever she was up to it seemed urgent, and he wished he knew what it was.

Through the gate they went, Archie breathlessly trying to keep pace with her, wondering what it was that was causing her to make such speed.

It would be something to do with the MacMorran brothers, he thought, the two who had tried to poach the river. But he thought that had all died down, barring poor old Dougal being taken to court for grievous bodily harm or something. No, it couldn't be that, of course. There was no such charge in Scotland. Assault with a deadly weapon, wasn't that it? He supposed that was not so serious as attempted murder.

They came down on to the shore and Archie found his feet slipping on the shingle while Mrs Cunningham didn't seem to be affected. She was able to stride out, straight and purposeful, while he floundered along behind like a rook with a broken wing. It really wasn't fair.

He caught up with her finally as she reached the barred and padlocked gate which led into the Ministry of Defence property at Laird's Point. By now the evening was well advanced, but the clear sky meant that the light was holding up longer than usual although it also meant that it was getting very cold indeed and there would probably be a heavy frost before morning.

"They've gone," said Mrs Cunningham.

Archie stopped beside her and nodded agreement. At the moment he wouldn't have been capable of speech.

There was certainly no sign of life within Laird's Point. Everything was shut and locked, a shroud over the engine of the bulldozer and a couple of lorries with Henderson and Speirs's insignia on them standing empty and idle. Mrs Cunningham gave vent to what sounded suspiciously like a swear word, though Archie couldn't be sure through the sound of his own heavy breathing.

"Where are they?" she asked.

"Gone back to Auchtarne," said Archie, finding words possible again at last.

"Yes, I suppose so," said Mrs Cunningham. "I hope so, anyway."

"Why, Mrs Cunningham?" asked Archie, managing to get out the question which had been bothering him ever since she had called at the flat over the stables.

"Because I think something's brewing, Archie," she said.

He thought the only thing that was brewing was the pot of tea on his cooker. It would be well and truly birsled by now . . .

"Beg pardon?" he said.

"They're planning something, Archie, and I want to find out what."

"You mean more poaching?"

"Something like that, yes."

"Och, no, Mrs Cunningham, they'll have had enough. There's Dougal put one of them out of action already. The other one won't be wanting the same thing happening to him."

"I'm not so sure. Come along, Archie. We must get back. If they're not here there are several telephone calls I must make. Find out exactly where the man is."

She turned and began to make her way back along the shingle, and Archie, with a sigh, turned and followed her.

Really, for all the good they'd done they might as well not have come and he could have stayed where he was and enjoyed his baked beans. And the tea . . . But now it sounded as though Mrs Cunningham was expecting him to do other things as well, and he thought gloomily that he'd be lucky if he saw a baked bean that night.

9

Mr Murdoch made his way down the track towards the road, walking carefully. Not that he was scared of tripping over a root, but he now carried incriminating evidence on him, and the thought made him very wary.

Mind you, in a way he was used to this. There were

people in the village who didn't understand his little expeditions into the wild every now and then and who might be inclined to place the wrong interpretation on them, so he had become accustomed to taking things very cautiously when out on the hill.

And this time it was just as well, because he became aware that he had company long before the other person became aware of him.

He heard the sound of a shoe on a stone some distance down the path he was on, and immediately he melted into the background of trees and bushes and stood quite still, waiting.

The light had almost gone now, and he knew that so long as he didn't move anyone on the path was most unlikely to spot him, though the temptation to sink deeper into shelter was very strong. But doing so might cause a twig to crack, and that would warn whoever was on the path that he was not alone.

He stood wishing his heart wouldn't pound quite so loudly. He was sure it must be audible to everyone within a radius of twenty yards or so, and trying to still it made him breathe more heavily too.

Dull footsteps approached, and a moment later between the trunks of two beech trees, Mr Murdoch saw a figure approaching round a bend in the track. He drew in a sharp but mercifully silent breath and watched as Joe MacMorran walked quietly past.

He knew it was Joe MacMorran without ever having seen him before. The description had been circulating round Glendarroch for days, and anyway strangers here at this time of year were most unusual. It had to be Joe MacMorran.

Was he going back to collect the incriminating evidence which Mr Murdoch now had concealed about his person? He began to wish he'd left it where it was. Supposing MacMorran reached the spot, found the handkerchief he'd left conspicuously tied to the bush and therefore found the evidence missing? Would he come down the track like an avenging angel, searching for the man who could give him away to the police?

Mr Murdoch shivered and wished he was at home sitting in front of the warm fire, a rabbit bubbling in the pot in the kitchen, Ben, his dog, stretched out asleep on the hearthrug and the television set tuned to some adventurous police thriller where awful things happened to other people but never to yourself.

But then common sense took over. Even if MacMorran found the handkerchief and then found that the evidence was no longer there, he had no idea how long it had been gone for, and wouldn't feel there was any point in leaping round the hill like a demented stag trying to find someone who was probably not there in the first place.

Slightly reassured, Mr Murdoch slipped back on to the track and turned to face down the slope towards the road.

And then a ghastly thought froze him to the track and when at last he forced himself to move he didn't set off downwards, away from the point of danger, but upwards, moving quickly but cautiously after MacMorran, cursing his stupidity in a manner which would have shocked his fellow members of the kirk session.

He was a good stalker, of course. There were those unkind enough in the village to say that he had more than enough practice at it, but a man who went out so often after vermin for the pot had to be, and he was sure he could follow MacMorran without MacMorran knowing he was there.

It wasn't bravado which made him do this. He wasn't really interested in where MacMorran was going. It was simply to reassure himself that MacMorran didn't find that tell-tale handkerchief so that he could rest easily in his bed, because the thought which had frozen him to the track was that he couldn't remember whether that handkerchief was one which had his initial on it or not. His sister in Aberdeen had sent him three initialled hankies for his birthday and he alternated them with his ordinary plain ones. If this was an initialled one it wouldn't matter if MacMorran thought he was around at the moment or not. He could probably trace him and murder him in his bed when he was asleep and helpless.

Mind you, an initialled handkerchief wasn't anything like positive identification but it was a great deal too close to it for comfort. And Obadiah was an unusual name.

At that moment he felt reassured by the pressure of the shotgun on his arm. If the worst came to the worst the

older brother might end up in hospital with the same
complaint as the younger one.

But if MacMorran didn't find the handkerchief, then at
least Mr Murdoch could rectify the mistake he had made
and take it away himself. He would recognise the spot
without the aid of a mark like that. He had been stupid to
do it in the first place. It all came from feeling too sorry for
Dougal Lachlan.

He saw the shadowy figure ahead of him and he allowed
it to keep ahead, not appearing himself on the path until
the figure had been carried round the next bend. In this
way his progress upwards was by a series of stops and
starts.

He came to the place where the track branched and a
glance up the branch which led towards the river and the
handkerchief showed that it was empty. MacMorran
hadn't gone that way after all, and Mr Murdoch breathed a
sigh of relief.

Peering cautiously along the other track he saw the
figure disappearing round the next bend and he himself
stopped. There was no point in going any further. The
handkerchief was safe.

And now reaction set in and he didn't want to spend
any more time on the darkening hillside alone with a
dangerous criminal. Even if MacMorran did a circuit and
came down by the river track, by the time he did so it
would be too dark to see the handkerchief anyway. He
could safely leave it where it was after all.

Mr Murdoch turned and hurried away down the track
again, satisfied that he was safe. But as he did so he found
himself wondering why MacMorran had taken the left-
ward track.

After all, that only led to the deer farm.

Chapter Five

1

"I'll be glad when Ken gets back," said Brian. "It's lonely up there on the haggs. No one to chat to when you're eating your piece. Jimmy back yet?"

Isabel glanced at the clock.

"Not yet. The ferry should be just about in now. He won't be a minute. Your tea's ready."

"Good. I'm starving. Nothing like the good open air life to give you an appetite."

"And keep your waist line down."

"True, true. And make you feel your back's been twisted into a granny knot."

He sank down into his chair with a groan and spread his feet out towards the fire.

"Ah, that's good. A can of beer, a plate of chips, and thou."

"Oh, aye, in that order, I suppose."

"Certainly. I always get my priorities right—"

The back door slammed open.

"Dad—?"

"Here, Jimmy," said Brian, and Jimmy appeared in the doorway from the kitchen, still in his oilskins and boots. He hadn't even stopped at the office to take them off. Brian sat up suddenly, sensing something wrong.

"What is it?" he asked.

"Trouble. The telephone lines are down between here and Auchtarne, so we can't get a message out. Ken thinks there's going to be an attack on the deer farm."

"What!"

"That's what he said. He'll be back himself shortly, but he asked me to put out a warning as soon as I got in."

"What makes him think that?"

Brian was on his feet, heading for the kitchen and the spot where he had left his boots. Isabel followed wordlessly.

"Four men in a land-rover stopped for petrol at Duff's Garage. And then they took the Glendarroch road. He's pretty sure one of them carried a sub-machine gun."

"Oh, no!" said Isabel, understanding immediately the implications of that.

"Just pretty sure?"

"He said he recognised the types. Small-time crooks from Glasgow he said."

Brian nodded as he slipped his feet into the boots.

"Ken would know. He spent some time amongst folk like that when he was in trouble with the drink. Okay. Jimmy. You take the van. Get up to Ardvain. Warn the crofters. Isabel—try the telephone. See if we can still make local calls. If so, warn as many people as you can. Mrs Cunningham, for one. Right, son?"

"Okay," said Jimmy. "Van keys?"

Brian pulled them out of his pocket and chucked them over to him. Jimmy hurried out into the yard and a moment later they heard the roar of the van engine start and then fade as he raced out of the yard on to the road, heading for the Ardvain track.

"Brian—take care," said Isabel anxiously.

"I will, I will," he said, fastening his anorak and searching the shelf for a torch as he did so.

"If Ken's right, and they have a sub-machine gun—"

"I know. The whole herd could go in a matter of minutes. We'll get the gang all right, no doubt about that. Saving the deer's another matter."

"And they might not just use the sub-machine gun on the deer," said Isabel.

He paused for a moment.

"I hadn't thought of that," he said.

"Well, think of it now," she said sharply.

"Yes. I am. And I'm also thinking of the deer and what that farm means to the whole estate. You realise if it goes Mrs Cunningham may well go bankrupt? She's got an awful lot of capital tied up in it."

"And I've got a lot of capital tied up in you and Jimmy," she said.

He took her in his arms and kissed her fiercely.

"It's all right," he said. "We can take care of ourselves. No yobbos from Glasgow are going to take pot shots at us."

He turned and left the kitchen before she could protest any further and set off out of the yard and along the road

which led towards the deer fence. He had felt stiff and
tired coming home from the peat cutting, his only thought
being of a good meal and an evening dozing in front of
the fire and the television set. Now the adrenalin was
pumping with the news Jimmy had brought, driving out
the ache in his bones and the general weariness, and as he
trotted along the road a sense of anger kept the adrenalin
pumping and he was quite glad of the need for activity.
There was still sufficient light to see where he was going,
but it would be gone in another quarter of an hour, long
before he reached the actual fence and, he hoped, even
longer before the gang reached it. As he went his mind,
having thrown off its lethargy, was busy with calculations.
The ferry took about a quarter of an hour less than the
road journey, for the road had to wind round the head of
the loch and was not made for speeding. With any luck he
would get there before they did. He didn't know what he
was going to do once he got there. It was an enormous
area to patrol on his own, literally miles of fence right
round the hill on which the deer farm was laid out, but at
least he would be there and could hold the fort until
reinforcements in the shape of a group of very angry
crofters arrived to help out.

2

Isabel frantically dialled the number of the manse and
waited tensely to see what happened. It had suddenly
come to her that the minister was going to Auchtarne that
evening to visit a parishioner in the cottage hospital, old
Mrs Farquhar who, so Mrs Mack had said, was not
expected to survive the night, which probably meant that
she would be out of the hospital hale and hearty by the
end of the week.

If that were so Mr MacPherson might be able to help, at
least by getting a message to the police.

She sighed with relief as the familiar comforting burr-
burr started at the other end. Clearly they could still make
local calls. The ringing tone went on for a while and then
the receiver was lifted and a suspicious voice said:

"Glendarroch Manse, who is this?"

"Mrs Mack, it's Isabel Blair. Is the minister there, please?"

"The minister has just left for Auchtarne," said Mrs Mack in the tone of a station announcer talking about a departing train, and Isabel's heart sank.

"Can't you stop him?" she asked.

"I can not. The car left the drive two minutes ago. He is on his way."

Mrs Mack was very formal on the telephone. She actually preferred addressing people face to face where she could watch them quail before her basilisk stare. There was no point in carrying on the conversation anyway.

"Oh, well. Thanks, Mrs Mack."

"Is anything wrong, Isabel?"

There was a sharpening of interest in her voice. Isabel wasn't sure how she did it, but she had an uncanny ability to detect trouble from the tone of people's voices.

"No. Not really. No. Just a wee panic, that's all."

"Panic helps no one, Isabel. A quiet mind makes a quiet life, as my Mr Mack used to always say . . ."

"Yes, I'm sure. Thanks, Mrs Mack. Good night . . ."

Isabel put the receiver down hurriedly before she could hear any more of the late Mr Mack's endless and pointless sayings and wondered what to do next. Catching Mr MacPherson before he left had been her big hope. Anything else seemed like anticlimax. But she started to dial again with a determined urgency. After all, her husband and her son seemed at the moment to be the only people who stood between this gang and the deer farm. She just hoped they wouldn't stand too obviously between them.

3

Joe MacMorran came down the track from the turning area to the gate at the road. His watch told him that it was about five minutes to rendezvous time and it wouldn't do for him to miss it. Prettyboy had worked out everything to the last minute and had stressed that timing was very important. He thought of The Progger and The Progger's favourite weapon and shivered slightly. It wasn't a sensation he enjoyed very much. With Stevie he had become used to being the boss, the one to give the orders and to plan the business, but he had to acknowledge that to carry out a scheme such as he had suggested to Prettyboy needed a lot more contacts and a lot more organisation than he was capable of himself, certainly when he was stuck in the back of beyond in a dump like this. But that didn't mean he had to like his new subordinate position.

He came down to the gate and into the shadow of the trees. It was now so dark that when he stepped beyond the gate and saw the vehicle standing there just in front of him he thought for a ghastly moment that he was late and that the land-rover had arrived before him.

It was a relief in a way to see that it was just an ordinary car, an ancient Mini by the look of it, but it was less of a relief to see that the bonnet was up and that there was a man peering rather helplessly into the dim interior.

The momentary relief vanished. Here was an unexpected problem. The land-rover was due any minute and this stranger was occupying the very spot the land-rover should be stopping in, ready to hear whatever was said. He'd have to get rid of him somehow, and he hoped it wouldn't have to be by violent means.

Even as he thought it the figure bending over the bonnet straightened up and Joe caught a glimpse of the whiteness round his neck which meant a dog collar. A ruddy God-merchant, he thought. That's the last thing I need.

The minister caught sight of him and gave a jump of surprise.

"Oh. Good evening," he said. "I'm sorry. I didn't know anyone was there. I wonder, do you know anything about motor car engines? I'm afraid my knowledge is sadly limited."

Joe took a deep breath and went into his helpful stranger routine.

"A bit, padre," he said cheerfully. "A wee bit. Did a joab in a garridge wance."

"You're a mechanic?"

"Got it in wan, padre. Got it in wan. Now what seems to be the trouble?"

The quickest way of getting rid of the old pest would be

to get him going again and out of here in double quick time. If that were possible. If not, he'd have to think again.

"Well, it's very strange. Usually I can't get the thing started, but once it starts it doesn't stop. You know. Even when I switch off."

"Touch of the post ignitions, padre," said Joe.

"Yes, yes, I daresay you're right," said the minister with the respect due to one who understood arcane subjects. "Well, this time it just stopped. Died on me, you might say. I was driving along and suddenly the engine cut out."

"Could be the points. Let's have a look, though. Stand back, padre, and let the cat see the rabbit."

He sat down in the driver's seat and switched on the lights. They came on strong, so there was nothing wrong with the battery. And in the dim glow of the dashboard light he saw what he had half-suspected and certainly hoped for. The fuel guage registered zero. He switched the lights off again.

"Quite a common occurrence, padre. Happens to the best of us. You're oot of juice."

"No petrol? Dear me, isn't that extraordinary! I thought there was ample to get me to Auchtarne. But there. I forgot. I had to go up to Ardvain yesterday and that is a very steep climb as perhaps you know. It probably used more than I had bargained for."

"Got a jerrycan?"

"Oh, yes. Certainly. There being no garage in Glendarroch now I never travel without one. It's in the boot."

Couldn't be easier, thought Joe, and he'd get rid of the old bird in plenty of time. The minister unlocked the boot and as he reached in for the jerrycan Joe glanced at his watch. Still a couple of minutes to go, and with any luck the rendezvous would be clear by then.

He poured petrol into the tank and then put the cap on the jerrycan again.

"There you are, padre. All topped up. Try her now."

The minister sat in the driving seat and switched on the ignition. The engine coughed and then sprang into life.

"Thank you so much," said the minister. "I am most grateful. Can I give you a lift anywhere? I'm going to Auchtarne if it's of any use to you . . ."

Joe had already deduced where he was going from the direction the car was pointing in, so he shook his head.

"Very kind of ye, padre, but I'm going the other way. Thanks all the same."

The minister looked slightly puzzled, wondering where a stranger would be going to in Glendarroch at this time of night, but since Joe didn't volunteer any information he was too polite and too grateful to ask.

"Well, thank you. As you say, the simplest things are often the most puzzling, aren't they? Good night."

"Good night, padre," said Joe, and watched as the minister carefully put the car into gear, switched on the indicator light to show that he was thinking about pulling out, glanced in his mirror, then over his shoulder and having finally decided that there wasn't another vehicle within half a mile of him, started off with a jerk and continued to jerk with increasing ferocity as the car gained speed.

Joe watched him go and then glanced at his watch again. Thank God the land-rover was actually late. Now at least the rendezvous was clear.

4

Mrs Mack put down the copy of *Life and Work* as she heard footsteps approach the back door of the kitchen and was already half way to opening it when the knock came.

It was a heavy knock, much heavier than Mr Murdoch's usual knock on these occasions and she tutted impatiently as she worked at the bolts, thankful that the minister was already on his way to Auchtarne and would not be disturbed by the noise and, possibly, come to see what was the cause.

She opened the door and Mr Murdoch, looking disgracefully hot and bothered, stumbled past her into the kitchen.

"You can not come in, Mr Murdoch," she said, scandalised. "I am alone. The minister is out."

But Mr Murdoch paid no attention. He simply staggered into the kitchen and sank down breathlessly at the kitchen table. Mrs Mack hesitated. Here was a fine dilemma!

Herself alone in the manse with a man—what would the people say? She could imagine the whispers behind the hands as she entered the Store or walked along the street. She whose moral behaviour was always beyond reproach!

"Will you please leave, Mr Murdoch?" she demanded, holding the door wide to let him make an exit.

But Mr Murdoch showed no sign of responding to her request and the cold air whirled into the kitchen and made her shiver, so with some reluctance she closed the door and went and sat as far away from Mr Murdoch as she could, having first made sure that the curtains at the window were firmly closed and that no one could possibly see through the smallest chink.

"Where is my rabbit?" she asked.

After a moment he felt in a pocket and a brown bundle landed softly on the well-scrubbed table top.

"Thank you. I am very grateful. I am sure the minister will be too, but as I said, he is not in at present . . ."

But still Mr Murdoch was not listening. He began to fumble in the other pocket of his overcoat and first a small square blue box landed on the table and then a large plastic bag, carefully folded in four . . . The box, she saw, was a battery, and the bag had lettering on it although from the way it was folded she could not make out what it said.

"What is all this?" she asked. "I scrubbed that table this morning, Mr Murdoch. I really don't think you should be putting your equipment on it at this time in the evening . . ."

Mr Murdoch seemed at last to be recovering and for the first time she found herself wondering why he should be so out of breath when he had merely been pursuing a course of action which was as familiar to him as breathing itself.

"Evidence," he said at last.

"Evidence?"

"Aye. Evidence."

"Are you feeling quite all right, Mr Murdoch? You look a little flushed. Can I get you something to drink?"

The last thing she wanted was for Mr Murdoch to have a heart attack at the kitchen table. That would involve summoning Nurse Semple and probably Dr Wallace as well, and then the news would be all round the village that Mr Murdoch had been here with her alone and people would wonder what had caused him to have a heart attack there and her reputation would be in ruins. She knew only too well how people in Glendarroch gossiped and exaggerated things.

"Do you—perhaps—have a drop of whisky?"

"Whisky?" she echoed, scarcely able to believe her ears.

"Purely for medicinal purposes—"

"Wine is a mocker, Mr Murdoch, as you very well know, and strong drink is raging. Proverbs twenty. This is the manse, Mr Murdoch, not a public hostelry."

"It's just that I've had rather a shock, Mrs Mack. In fact," he added with considerable feeling, "I've had a hell of a shock."

"Mr Murdoch!"

"I beg your pardon. It's the force of my emotion, Mrs Mack. I do beg your pardon."

He looked down at the two objects on the table and remained still for quite some time. She could see that he was thinking very deeply, and realised that something had happened to cause him considerable fright.

She began to wonder what it was. What had happened to him? What had he seen? What scandal was he in the process of uncovering?

"Tell me about it," she said, nostrils already quivering.

"Evidence, Mrs Mack. Evidence that those two men Dougal Lachlan shot at were indeed poaching."

Mrs Mack experienced a profound sense of disappointment. Not only had Mr Murdoch not uncovered some new scandal in the village, but he seemed to be doing his best to lay to rest an old one.

"I don't believe it," she said.

"It's true. I found those about three hundred yards from Peddie's Pool, hidden under some bushes."

"I don't understand how that proves that the men were poaching."

"The bag, woman, the bag!"

He picked it up and shook it out and then stabbed a trembling finger at the lettering.

"See there. Henderson and Speirs. The firm those two men work for. They took the bag with them to put the fish they hoped to take in."

"But the battery?"

"The battery was used to set off the explosion, don't you see? And I'll bet if the police go over the place with a fine tooth comb they'll find further evidence there. Oh, Lord."

"What is it?"

"It's just that after I'd found this stuff I nearly bumped into one of the men. I'm sure it was one of them."

Mrs Mack sat down again opposite him. This might not be a scandal. But it was the next best thing. A thrill.

"Did he see you?"

"Mercifully no, Mrs Mack. Mercifully no. If he had I doubt if I should be here now in such distress and state of thirst as you cannot imagine."

She got up.

"I shall put the kettle on," she said firmly.

"Aye. Aye, I'm sure that would be most welcome," he said, though his tone of voice betrayed little enthusiasm. "Do you think I might use the telephone?"

"What for?"

"To ring the police in Auchtarne, of course. They should know about this as soon as possible."

Mrs Mack considered. She didn't have to pay the telephone bills, but the minister did and she knew his stipend was not large. He was sparing of the telephone himself, but did not stint its use by others, something she frequently had cause to remonstrate with him about, but in this case it did seem important that Mr Murdoch should be allowed to use it.

"This way, please," she said, making up her mind that the minister would approve, and she led him from the kitchen into the hall where the telephone stood on a little table near the study door.

She waved at it, inviting him to make use of it, and then retired into the kitchen again. She didn't wait behind to listen. After all, it was one thing having a man in the kitchen. Quite another to have him in the hall. It was difficult to know where such a progression might end. But she remembered to leave the door wide open.

As she set about the preparations for a nice cup of tea she listened carefully. She heard the telephone being dialled. Then the receiver went down and the dialling started again. She waited to hear what was said, but there was no sound of speech. A little later Mr Murdoch returned to the kitchen.

"I keep getting the unobtainable signal," he said. "Is there something the matter with your phone?"

"Certainly not," said Mrs Mack indignantly, taking the suggestion as a personal affront.

"Then there's something wrong with the line. I can't get through to Auchtarne at all."

"It's a judgement," said Mrs Mack.

"Eh?"

"A judgement. Glendarroch is an evil place, Mr Murdoch, as you and I know only too well. Full of immorality and intrigue and lust. Now we find there is further immorality in the persons of these men who were poaching."

She felt indignation rising in her. She herself had spoken at length to one of the men, the one who had been in the church. Oh, he had been plausible. Very plausible indeed. He had taken her in, all right, and she flattered herself that there weren't many people who could do that. But she saw now that he had been as false as hell. Yes, indeed, he was the devil himself come straight from hell, and she in her Christian charity and care had befriended him and taken him to her bosom—well, figuratively speaking, of course—and now this was how Christian virtue was to be repaid.

"I don't quite see how losing the telephone to Auchtarne is a judgement, Mrs Mack," said Mr Murdoch.

"Oh, you may not see it, Mr Murdoch. But I assure you everything is meant. And that is a judgement."

"Well, maybe—"

"God has sent it to us as a punishment for the wickedness of this place, Mr Murdoch, and there is nothing we can do but accept it."

"Oh, but you're always saying that God helps those who help themselves, Mrs Mack."

That stopped her for a moment, but only for a moment.

"Are you suggesting that we can go against God's will by going out and repairing the telephone lines, Mr Murdoch?" she asked with biting sarcasm.

"No, but—"

"I'm glad to hear it."

"But I'm not convinced he's asking us to sit back and do nothing about it. Now, if I had a car I could drive into Auchtarne and deliver these things to Sergeant Murray—"

"But you have no car. That, too, is meant."

Mr Murdoch sighed.

"Well, if you say so, Mrs Mack," he said.

"I do," said Mrs Mack, bringing the discussion to a firm close as she ladled tea into the teapot. He really did look rather distressed so in generosity of spirit she put a third spoonful into the pot as an extra.

5

Mr MacPherson moved carefully into second gear and achieved it without that distressing grinding of metal which such action usually provoked. Relieved, he released his left foot from the clutch too quickly and the car jerked and hit him in the back.

After that it was better. He wondered why changing gears got progressively easier the higher they went. A few seconds later when he moved into top he achieved it really remarkably smoothly.

He took the car to the top speed at which he felt it was safe to drive on this road and in these conditions, and proceeded at twenty miles an hour in the direction of Auchtarne.

It was as well he was going no faster. As he approached a really rather dangerous bend another vehicle proceeding in the opposite direction came round with no headlights on and nearly drove him into the ditch. He peeped the horn indignantly and carried on as the vehicle swept past him and, glancing in his mirror he saw its tail lights disappearing towards Glendarroch.

Really, you weren't safe on any road these days, he thought. Had he been travelling any faster that irresponsible fool might well have run into him.

An increase of red light in the mirror showed him that the vehicle was slowing and in fact, just as he went into the bend and the view behind was cut off by the hedge, he was sure he saw it stopping where he had stopped. But he had no time to watch more closely. Steering round this bend was a remarkably tricky job. Perhaps the man who had helped him so efficiently had flagged it down and was hitching a lift into Glendarroch, he thought.

But the minister's adventures weren't over for the night. About half a mile further on, in the glow of his headlights, a figure suddenly appeared in the middle of the road waving its arms, signalling him to stop.

For a moment he wondered whether he should drive on. The figure looked a little demented. It might not be safe to stop. But perhaps the creature, whoever it was, needed help, so he carefully ensured that his door was locked and that the window was firmly closed. Better safe than sorry, he told himself. If there was any threat he trusted to being able to get the car to move away sufficiently fast to avoid being set upon, though frankly he doubted his ability to perform such a feat of mechanical competence.

He stopped a few feet from the figure, which came towards the door. Mr MacPherson lowered the window a fraction so that conversation could take place.

"Can I help you?" he asked.

"Minister—glad to see you," said a familiar voice, and Mr MacPherson wound the window right down.

"Mr Blair," he said. "Come in. I'll give you a lift."

"Thanks, Minister, but I'd better stay here. Listen. Have you passed a land-rover?"

"I have overtaken nothing—"

"No, going the other way."

"Oh. Well, I have certainly just passed a vehicle of some kind. It very nearly forced me off the road. Just at that last bend which I always consider to be one of the most dangerous in Argyll—"

"Was it a land-rover?"

"I'm afraid one vehicle is very like another to me, Mr Blair, not being of a mechanical turn of mind. Especially in the dark . . ."

That sounded rather as though he might prove a reasonable mechanic in daylight which was not the impression he intended to convey.

"Sort of set high on the road and square shaped," suggested Brian Blair.

"Possibly. Yes, very possibly."

"Then they're through."

"Who are through?"

"Poachers, we think, Mr MacPherson."

"Dear me. Another lot?"

"Well, possibly part of the same lot. Did the land-rover stop at all, or did it go on towards Glendarroch?"

"Well, I can't be sure, but I got the impression that it may have stopped just where the access track goes up towards Corrie Vrannichan. It was just at that point that I met a most helpful young man when I ran out of petrol—"

"What did he look like, this young man?"

"Well, I scarcely noticed. It was quite dark, you know."

"Mr MacPherson, you're going to Auchtarne?"

"Yes. I promised to visit old Mrs Farquhar in the hospital this evening—"

"Could you do something for us?"

"Certainly, if I can."

"We believe the telephone line's down between Glendarroch and Auchtarne, and we can't get through."

"Dear me, how inconvenient. It keeps happening, I'm afraid—"

"Could you call at the police station and tell Sergeant Murray we believe there's going to be an attack on the deer farm and that we urgently need help?"

"Good gracious, are you sure?"

"I'm not sure about the attack, but I think so, and if there is one then I'm sure we'll need help."

"Yes. Yes, of course I will. I shall go there straightaway. I may miss the visiting hour at the hospital and Mrs Farquhar will be most disappointed. She relies on me to keep her up to date with all that is happening in Glendarroch, you know—"

"Then you'll have a lot to tell her next time, Minister."

"Indeed I will. Very well, Mr Blair, you may leave it to me. I shall report to the police station as soon as I get there."

"Thank you."

"And Mr Blair—"

"Aye?"

"I hope you're wrong."

"So do I, Minister. So do I."

He stepped back and Mr MacPherson hunted for first

gear and, after wiggling the stick for a few moments, found it. Very carefully with that left foot now, he thought, and a moment later the car jerked violently and began to move down the road.

6

The telephone was ringing as Archie followed Mrs Cunningham into the hall.

"Answer that, will you, Archie?" she said, and he hurried through into the reception room where the machine was summoning him. Answer it, he thought. What with? He hardly had any breath left after that useless trip down to Laird's Point. And he'd spent all that day and a lot of the previous one tidying up the kitchen garden, and Mrs Cunningham hadn't even noticed. It really was a very hard and unrewarding life.

He lifted the receiver.

"Glendarroch Estates," he panted.

"Archie—it's Isabel."

"Hallo, Isabel. How are you? Haven't seen you for a wee whilie."

"I'm fine, Archie. Listen, is Mrs Cunningham there?"

"Aye, she's here. We've just come in—"

"Aye, I've been trying and trying and not getting an answer."

"That's funny. Fiona's around somewhere. Och, here, the telephone wasna switched through to the flat. She'll not have heard it. I should have done that before we went out, but to tell you the truth I didna really have the time to think about it . . . Here's Mrs Cunningham, Isabel."

Mrs Cunningham had come in behind him and he handed the receiver over to her, mouthing "Isabel Blair" as he did so.

Mrs Cunningham took the receiver from him.

"Hallo, Isabel," she said. "Yes . . . Yes . . ."

Archie saw her frown suddenly and then she said sharply:

"Just a moment, Isabel, please." And she turned to him. "Archie. Go through to the office. Listen on the extension."

Archie stared but the order was crisp and decisive so he

hurried through to the factor's office and raised the receiver on the desk. Isabel's voice came through to him.

". . . a land-rover with four men in it and Ken thinks one of them has a sub-machine gun. He thinks they're heading for the deer farm."

"The police—" He heard Mrs Cunningham's voice strangely coming from the receiver and through the open door at the same time.

"The line's broken between here and Auchtarne again. We can't get a message through. But Ken will have gone to them so there should be help coming soon. But we don't know when, and of course we don't know whether they'll come just on Ken's say-so. He's got nothing to go on except suspicion."

"So it's up to us, isn't it?" said Mrs Cunningham.

"I think it is. Jimmy's gone to warn the crofters around Ardvain and Brian's out keeping an eye on the deer fence, but we're awful thin on the ground . . ."

"Thank you for letting me know, Isabel. At least *we* can keep in touch by telephone."

"You think Ken may be right, Mrs Cunningham?"

"I'm sure he's right, Isabel. I've had confirmation from another source that something is brewing. I wish we could get in touch with Ken to tell him to pass it on to the police . . ."

"If you could get in touch with Ken you could get in touch with the police yourself direct."

"Of course I could. I'm afraid I'm not thinking straight at the moment, Isabel. I'll get off the line and let you make any other calls you think necessary. Forget about the police. I'll keep trying them every five minutes from here. With any luck the line will be restored before too long, and at least we can be sure they know the full facts as soon as possible. I'm not very sure that there's much else we women can do."

"Right, Mrs Cunningham. Cheerio now."

There was a click and the line went dead.

Archie replaced the receiver with a hand which trembled slightly. A sub-machine gun, for heaven's sake . . . He didn't like the idea of facing anything like that . . .

Mrs Cunningham appeared in the doorway, looking a little pale. He watched her with sympathy. She'd sunk a lot of money into the deer farm, he thought. Far more than she could really afford. Was it all going to be wiped away in a single night?

Not if he could help it.

"You needing the car, Mrs Cunningham?" he asked.

She brought herself back to the present with a start and shook her head.

"I think I'd better just stay here," she said.

"Right."

She stood aside to let him pass as he headed determindedly for the door.

"Where are you going?" she asked.

"To help," he said.

He selected a key from the keyboard behind Lorna's desk and marched across the hall. He unlocked a door which led into one of the unused wings of the house. Down here had been the billiard room and the smoking room, and beyond it the conservatory. In the old days there had been the click of billiard balls and the heady smell of cigar smoke and the clink of glasses in the evening, the days when there had been shooting and fishing parties throughout the year and the house had thronged with elegant folk who dressed in Highland dress for dinner and took part in eightsome reels in the stone-flagged hallway with its hammer beam rafters, while the bagpipes skirled and echoed round the stone walls.

Those days were gone, he thought, as he passed down the dusty corridor, feeling a cobweb brush his face as he went. Dim bare bulbs lit the stone floor and the walls from which the plaster was showing signs of peeling and there was a smell of damp. Maybe he would have to do something about all this one day. But not just now.

And there on the wall, between a faded oil-painting of a Highland landscape which might have been by Landseer and a grim portrait of some long-forgotten Peddie, was what he was looking for.

When Archie drove away from Glendarroch House there sat on the passenger seat a heavily ornamented blunderbuss dating from 1788 with a horn at the end of the barrel like a trumpet bell. It hadn't been fired for well over a hundred years and would probably never fire

again, but Archie felt a great deal more secure having it on
the seat beside him.

7

Brian watched the tail lights of the minister's Mini
meander down the middle of the road and vanish
uncertainly round the next bend. He shook his head
impatiently. The way the minister drove it would be nearly an hour before he got to the police station at
Auchtarne and he wondered how long it would then be
before he could persuade the police to take action. Of
course, the sight of the dog collar should be enough for
Sergeant Murray to accept his story at face value, but how
long would it take Murray to assemble a force and proceed
to Glendarroch? Another hour, maybe? Probably longer.
And that was assuming that Murray acted immediately.
There was no guarantee of that.

He turned and hurried back towards Glendarroch. It
was annoying that he had come down from the fence too
far along the road and the land-rover had slipped through.
But at least he knew it *was* through, and probably it was
just as well he hadn't met up with it. The thought of four
men and a sub-machine gun was slightly daunting.

The little indentation in the road where the gate in the
fence stood was empty when he got there. Not that he had
expected it to be anything else.

The light had strengthened now as a gibbous moon
swung up over the trees, but it wasn't bright enough to
see whether the tracks in the softer ground beyond the
gate were recent or not. He felt reasonably sure, though,
that that was where the land-rover had gone.

If only they had some means of communication, he
thought. A walkie-talkie would have been invaluable. All
he could do was keep an eye on the time and guess.

Jimmy had been away for nearly an hour and a quarter.
That meant that he should have passed the lower crofts
and by now should have reached as far as Ardvain. The
crofters wouldn't take long to respond to the call, so even
now they should be heading down that sheep track on the
other side of the road towards Glendarroch, grim-faced,
determined that the work which all of them had put in to

erect the deer fence and establish the farm should not be wasted.

He wished he'd arranged a rendezvous with Jimmy before he left, but they hadn't so all he could do was roam the fence, trying to spot the men when they arrived, trying to establish contact with the crofters as they got here.

Generally at the moment he saw his job as holding a watching brief. No more. Once the reinforcements came they would need to form a plan of action.

Though what sort of action they could take in the face of a sub-machine gun he wasn't sure.

8

They walked up the track in single file, Joe leading the way, Prettyboy following, then The Progger carrying the sub-machine gun cradled in his arms as though it was a wean, then Dracula, because you could never be sure that Dracula wouldn't get lost, and lastly Scruffy.

Joe had done well, thought Prettyboy appreciatively. In spite of the stop at the garage for petrol the rendezvous had been made without any fuss at all, and if what Joe had said was true, that stop might have been made because a good angel or something was watching over them, for if they'd come straight through they'd have landed at the rendezvous just when the God-merchant was sitting there and that could have spoilt the whole thing.

They'd brought the land-rover up the track to the turning place and stopped there. Joe had explained the strategy behind the choice.

"We get the refrigerator van up here," he'd said. "It should make that lower track no bother, and there's room for it to turn here and wait. No one'll see it from the road, even in the moonlight."

"I dinna like the moonlight," Dracula had complained. "Be better withoot it. In the daurk."

"And then hoo are we gonna see the beasts to get at them, ye eejit?" Prettyboy had enquired, and Dracula had subsided.

Joe had guided the land-rover further up the next track, its aged shock absorbers groaning with the effort as they shuddered and twisted, sometimes angled towards the sky so that nothing but a vehicle with four-wheel drive could have made it. They'd hidden it near the top in a little clearing Joe had found where all they had to do was drive through a screen of bushes and stop. It wasn't very good for the land-rover's paintwork, but the paintwork wasn't very good anyway, so that didn't matter.

Then they'd come up to the gate, but when Dracula stepped forward with the pliers, eager to cut the padlock, Joe had stopped him.

"No this wan," he'd said. "Roond the fence a wee bit."

"How no this wan?" Dracula had asked.

"Because for wan thing we'll be nearer the beasts through the next wan, and for another wance ye start firing yon thing there may be folk'll hear ye. This gate's the obvious wan to start investigations at."

Prettyboy had nodded approvingly and followed Joe round the hill, moving parallel with the line of the fence towards the next gate. Joe had explained in Glasgow that the deer farm was divided into different sections, all fenced off, so that the deer could be moved from one section to another and the grazing could recover in a used section. Not that that mattered at this time of year, but in the summer, when the beasts weren't fed by human hand, it did. Joe had really done his homework, he thought, and he was going to earn his share of the reward.

And the reward should be pretty hefty. He'd made enquiries before he'd finally set up the project, working out exactly what they could get, and Scruffy had known a man who had a friend whose cousin was in the wholesale meat trade, had connexions in the catering business, and wasn't too fussy about where his raw materials came from, and he'd struck a bargain with him. Working it out, it was a pretty fair one all round.

Venison fetched well over a pound a pound in the shops just now. There would be a hundred pounds weight on each beast, and the farm held over a hundred animals. That meant more than ten thousand pounds. Not that they'd get that, of course. Price to the trade would be about two thirds, and that was a legitimate price. To give Scruffy's friend's friend's cousin a decent cut they'd have to settle for a price of five thousand. Still, between the five of them that was a fair return for a night's work.

Joe stopped and the others gathered round.

"There's the gate," he said.

Just ahead, silver in the moonlight, they saw the gate, firmly padlocked, and Dracula flexed his pliers in anticipation.

"Fine," said Prettyboy. "Ye done well, Joe. I'm pleased. Very pleased."

"Thought ye'd like it, Prettyboy."

"I do, I do. Now, we'll take it from here, right? You nip back to the road and meet the van. It should be here in— he peered at the dial of his watch—"aboot forty minutes. Right?"

"Aye," said Joe.

"I just thought of something," said Dracula with a note of surprise in his voice.

"What's that, Dracula?" asked Prettyboy patiently. It was as well to listen to Dracula, even if you didn't pay attention to him, otherwise he got frustrated and started to bend things.

"How's Joe gonna reckernise the right van?"

Prettyboy sighed.

"Dracula, there's no gonna be awful many refrigerator vans on that road at this time of night, now is there? We're no exactly on the M8 motorway, are we?"

"No, that's true," said Dracula. "It's no the M8, so it's no."

"My feet are killing me," said Scruffy. "I wish we could have brung the land-rover all the way."

"We couldna do that," said Joe.

"I dinna see why no."

"The engine would frighten the beasts, ye ninny," said Prettyboy. "You ken what you're here for, Scruffy."

"I thought I was just here to drive. These big joabs, the driver usually just drives."

"I tellt ye, ye're here to help carry the beasts to the land-rover and then drive the land-rover down to the van when it gets here. This whole operation's got to go like clockwork, right?"

Scruffy sighed and said no more, perhaps feeling that he'd done enough to establish his presence.

"Off ye go then, Joe. See ye doon there."

"Aye, okay, Prettyboy. See ye."

Joe slipped away and disappeared between the trees, and then Prettyboy turned to Dracula.

"Right," he said.

Dracula grinned and stepped forward. Two seconds later the padlock fell away and Dracula and Scruffy pushed open the gates. They slipped in one by one and then pulled the gates to behind them.

Before they went on into the depths of the deer farm The Progger paused. Carefully he unzipped the canvas cover round the Sterling-Patchett and folded it and stuffed it into the front of his anorak. Then, assembling the stock and barrel, he licked his lips and nodded at Prettyboy.

Silently they began to move forward.

9

It was eight o'clock when Dougal arrived at the Glendarroch Store and as he had almost the furthest to come he found most of the others already waiting in the living room behind the shop. Isabel had got out Brian's bottle and most of them had drams in their hands.

"Not too much of that, now," he said. "We'll need all our wits about us."

"Jimmy?" asked Isabel anxiously.

"He went on to the Moncurs. They should be here in about a quarter of an hour or so," said Dougal.

In spite of his strictures he accepted a dram from Isabel and downed it in one, feeling the comforting glow spread through him. The others were looking at him, expecting leadership, perhaps because of the reputation he had gained for shooting one of the poachers already, he thought. Bob Taylor sat in Brian's chair opposite the television set. Hector MacNeill glowered in a corner, Inverdarroch stood fidgetting uncertainly from one foot to the other in front of the fireplace, Jamie Stewart was sitting in the deep chair, his grey beard jutting truculently. And there were others too: Archie, carrying something which looked as if it had been stolen from a museum and which might not have frightened a poacher but terrified the daylights out of Dougal.

None of the others carried a weapon of any kind. That was interesting. They knew about what had happened to him at Peddie's Pool and the consequent threat which was hanging over him for taking the law into his own hands at a time when the law itself couldn't have done a damned thing about it. They didn't want similar charges brought against them. He understood that attitude. In fact, with some reluctance, he approved of it. When Jimmy had called at Ardvain and blurted out the story Dougal had automatically gone for his shotgun.

But Grace had been adamant.

"You're in enough trouble with that thing already," she had said. "You'll only make it worse taking it with you again."

And reluctantly he had agreed with her and left it behind. After all, if what Jimmy said was true, it was quite likely that the police would actually be there this time and if there were all that many people around he didn't want to be up in court on a charge of potting Sergeant Murray by mistake.

"Is that thing loaded?" he asked Archie.

"No," said Archie. "But it'll make a fine club."

They all seemed to be waiting for him and Dougal wondered what on earth to do. This sort of situation was one which he had thought of occasionally ever since they had set up the deer farm, but having to face it and take immediate and effective action was a different matter entirely. He felt a bit at a loss.

"I think maybe we'd better not wait for the others," he said. "Time's important. Maybe Isabel can send them after us. If the poachers get to the farm they could be out again in ten minutes and we'll be helpless."

"What do we do, Dougal?" asked Inverdarroch.

Desperately he put his mind to it. They were relying on him for a plan. And gradually his mind began to move into gear.

"We'll need to put a guard right round the fence," he said.

There was an uncomfortable stir.

"That's a big, big area," said Jamie Stewart.

"I know, I know. But the gates are the most important things."

"Fifteen of them," said McNeill.

"Aye."

"And how many of us?"

Dougal did a rapid head count and there weren't enough. Seven in the room. He had just spotted Murdoch skulking in the background. Well, set a poacher to catch a poacher, he thought. The two Moncurs and Jimmy were on their way. Ken Calder would make eleven, but he wasn't here yet either. And somewhere out there was Brian, patrolling the fence himself at the moment. That was twelve. Which meant three gates would go unguarded.

Well, he could reduce the odds a bit. The three gates furthest up the hillside he could probably forget about. The poachers were likely to take the easiest route, not only because they were from the city and wouldn't be at home on the rough ground, but also because they would be anxious to have the shortest possible route for a quick getaway with the carcasses.

It was funny how his mind was beginning to work, accepting new information, rejecting the less feasible alternatives, making the most of the forces at his disposal.

Rapidly he began to spell out who would be responsible for which gate, saying that they should centre their efforts on the gates themselves but make a survey of the perimeter fence in each direction whenever they felt it were possible. He thought their ears would be as important as their eyes for this job.

"If you find them, shout your heads off," he said. "So long as they're outside the fence that'll scare them off. And it'll bring help. But watch it. Remember there's a submachine gun out there."

"We're not sure of that, though, are we?" said Archie hopefully.

"Well, don't try to prove it," said Dougal.

They didn't need reminding, though, and from the look in Archie's face, he didn't either. He watched as one by one the crofters left to take up their positions.

The Moncurs arrived as they were moving out and Jimmy came close behind with the Store van. Rapidly Dougal explained what they were to do. The Moncurs, who lived far away round Ben Darroch and who rarely

ever reached even such a point of civilisation as Glendarroch, looked slightly bewildered, but relieved not to
have to spend too long in the metropolis. They were more
at home out in the wild where they were heading
straightaway, shepherded by Dougal, without benefit of a
dram from Brian's bottle.

But the fact that they were out of their element here
gave Dougal a great deal of comfort. They would know
what they were doing out in the darkness of the slope of
the hill. The poachers probably didn't. Perhaps the odds
weren't stacked against them too much after all, in spite of
that sub-machine gun.

Dougal and Bob left in Dougal's land-rover accompani-
ed by Jimmy, and ten minutes later they were driving
slowly up the track towards the first gate where Dougal
intended to set up whatever sort of headquarters he could.

The track petered out some distance from this gate and
he drew to a halt when even the four-wheel drive
wouldn't take them any further. He stopped the engine
and switched off the lights and they climbed out and stood
for a moment, letting their eyes get accustomed to the
moonlight after the glare of the headlights.

"Right," said Dougal. "Let's move."

"It all seems terribly quiet," said Bob.

"Aye," said Dougal. "It does. Bob, you go to gate fifteen.
Patrol westwards from there. You'll meet up with Hamish
McNeill who's on the next gate."

Bob nodded and melted away through the trees silently
and swiftly. Dougal looked round. It all seemed peaceful
and slightly unearthly in the silver glow from the moon,
the contrast between light and shade very strong indeed,
but with shade predominating.

"What do we do now, Dougal?" asked Jimmy.

"We try gate one," said Dougal, and began to lead the
way through the bushes towards their objective. "And just
pray that they haven't got inside already," he added over
his shoulder.

10

Elizabeth put the receiver down.

"Still nothing," she said.

She got up and went to the window of the sitting room, gazing out at the moonlit garden below. There was a restlessness in her which she found difficulty in controlling, but she knew she had to, that there was no place for her out there in the dark. That was a man's world just now, and there was danger there. But she felt responsible for those people who would be gathering round the deer farm, the crofters and the folk from the village, all of whom were her people, she felt. They were doing this for her, because they knew what the deer farm meant to her. Of course they knew too that if the farm failed then they would fail as well, and she shuddered when she thought of what might happen to the estate if the poachers were successful tonight.

It had been a struggle to keep the estate going. She had fought off unscrupulous builders and unscrupulous businessmen and unscrupulous German financiers. Yes, and one or two unscrupulous landowners as well. Surely a handful of unscrupulous poachers wasn't going to pose anything like the same sort of threat?

But she knew they could, that what they planned was simple and fast and as far as the estate was concerned very deadly indeed.

They simply must not be allowed to succeed, and yet she had to sit here and let others do the work for her.

She swung back to the telephone and dialled again.

Fiona sat on the chair opposite her, bolt upright, hands clasped in her lap, watching her anxiously. Anxiously. That was good. That was an emotion. Had the tide turned there at least? It was possible.

The high pitched buzz.

She put the receiver down again.

"Nothing?" asked Fiona.

Elizabeth shook her head.

"Would you like some coffee?" asked Fiona.

"You know, I think I would."

Fiona got up and passed her on the way to the door. Impulsively Elizabeth put out a hand to stop her.

"Thank you, darling," she said quietly.

Fiona looked at her almost blankly, and she wondered if she had gone too far too quickly, but after a minute Fiona nodded, smiled slightly and then passed on.

Elizabeth paced the room a couple of times. I'll do that three times more and then try again, she told herself, forcing herself not to hurry the pace, to step slowly, take the full width of the room, step slowly back to the opposite wall, turn and do the same thing all over again. Three times she did it and then picked up the receiver and dialled again.

Clicks on the line, the same sort of clicks she had heard every time up till now . . .

Burr-burr . . . Burr-burr . . .

"Fiona!" she shouted. "We're through—!"

She heard a clatter from the kitchen and sensed Fiona return to the sitting room door as the receiver at the other end was lifted and a familiar voice said:

"Auchtarne police."

"Sergeant Murray. Thank God. Elizabeth Cunningham, Glendarroch House."

"Mrs Cunningham. Hallo. The line's back then. Yes, I knew it was down. I have had Ken Calder here telling me a strange tale about poachers."

"I think it's probably true, Sergeant. I've had confirmation from another source."

"What source would that be, Mrs Cunningham?"

Elizabeth glanced up at Fiona in the doorway. Obviously she could hear Sergeant Murray's voice from there because she nodded.

"My daughter," said Elizabeth. "She tells me that Stephen MacMorran told her this afternoon that his brother was planning something." She caught Fiona's appealing look, so she added: "Though he didn't know what it was and is clearly not involved himself."

"I see. Well, it all sounds a bit circumstantial, Mrs Cunningham. You'll understand it's not easy for me to summon many men on such slight evidence as this . . ."

Elizabeth sighed. Somehow she had thought that once they could establish contact with the police all their problems would be over. But that was far from the case, of course.

"Eh—would you hold on a minute please, Mrs Cunningham?"

She heard the sound of a hand being put over the

receiver and then the muffled sound of questions being asked which she couldn't hear properly. It seemed to go on for a long time and she began to feel impatience rising in her again. Then the hand was removed and Sergeant Murray spoke to her.

"Mrs Cunningham, I've just got Mr MacPherson here, and he is telling me that he has a message from Brian Blair who asked him to call here with some information. Mr Blair asserts that the gang is already in Glendarroch and may be at this moment approaching the deer farm."

"Oh, God . . ." said Elizabeth and then fell silent, not knowing what else there was to say. At the other end Murray too was silent and she wondered what was going on in his mind.

"Look, Mrs Cunningham," he said at last. "I'm going to put out a call for reinforcements but it'll be a long time before I can get any. Meanwhile, a couple of constables and I will be on our way to Glendarroch in about ten minutes."

Elizabeth closed her eyes in relief.

"Thank you, Sergeant," she said.

"I just hope we shall be in time," said Murray, and the line went dead.

11

Dougal kept the flashlight trained on the fence as he and Jimmy made their way round it towards the gate.

He shrugged deeper into his anorak. The temperature was plummeting now and must already be well below freezing point. It was a steely world they were in, without warmth or colour, everything black and white and in sharp contrast in the cold moonlight. The stars were very clear in the sky, and directly overhead stretched the broad irregular belt of the Milky Way, diffuse and mysterious with unimaginable distance.

Beside him Jimmy slipped slightly. A thin film of ice was already spangling the puddles left by the earlier rain.

They came to the next gate where Jimmy was to take up his post. Dougal would head for the following one which was the main gate up from the turning circle and the road beyond.

"If you see anything, shout," muttered Dougal and Jimmy nodded. "But not before you've put a couple of good stout trees between you and them. You'll probably terrify the daylights out of them, and we don't know how nervous the man's finger will be on that gun."

Dougal's torch was playing over the closed gates and suddenly came to a stop. Jimmy heard him swear under his breath. Dougal hurried forward and brought the torch to bear on the point where the two gates met. Then the torch light travelled downwards to the ground and Jimmy saw what had attracted his attention.

On the ground at the foot of the gates lay the padlock. In the torchlight they could see the curve of the lock had been sheared apart by a pair of very strong pliers.

"So," said Dougal. "We'll not need to guard the perimeter fence after all. They're inside already."

Chapter Six

1

Mrs Mack looked at the clock on the kitchen wall and frowned to herself. Time was moving very slowly.

The minister was unlikely to be back for an hour at least, knowing how Mrs Farquhar would keep him gossiping, and Mr Murdoch had left with his evidence more than half an hour ago. That had been unfortunate. It had given her too much time to think about things, to grow more and more indignant about the low state of morality into which Glendarroch was gradually sinking.

Not even gradually, she thought with some satisfaction. It seemed to her that the process was very fast indeed.

Yet in her growing and proper indignation at this state of affairs which, in spite of her own constant vigilance and oft-repeated warnings, seemed never to show signs of improvement, there was a tiny niggle at the back of her mind.

Take care of the pennies and the pounds will take care of themselves was a phrase which her Mr Mack used to always employ, and like all his little sayings there was a great deal of truth in it. It was unwise to consider that particular one as referring to a purely financial theme. One should also consider it in other ways. Perhaps that little niggle of thought at the back of her mind was one of the pennies which she should take care of.

And the penny which niggled at her was yet another phrase of Mr Mack's which Mr Murdoch had repeated right here in this very kitchen not much more than half an hour ago, attributing it to herself.

God helps those who help themselves.

Mrs Mack sat down in one of the hard chairs at the kitchen table and thought long and hard about that.

Was she perhaps being a little unjust in so roundly condemning the moral slide of Glendarroch when she did so little to stem that moral slide herself? Oh, true, she did her best with little words of advice, but it was strange how rarely people paid attention to them. Should her efforts not be turned into a more practical direction? If she began to take aan active personal interest in the affairs of Glendarroch, started a crusade like that nice Mr Billy Graham used to conduct so splendidly . . . She remember- ed going with Mr Mack to one of Mr Graham's crusades in the Kelvin Hall in Glasgow many years ago. It had been a thrilling experience and she and Mr Mack had shared a most uplifting spiritual revival and, as far as she was concerned, some of that thrill had never left her. Poor Mr Mack, of course, had not very long afterwards passed on to the place where spiritual revival was no longer necessary because, being always there it didn't need revival, but without his constant support and encourage- ment she was forced to undertake the task of spreading Mr Graham's torch into the dark places.

But Mr Graham too had gone out and laboured mightily for the message which he had to deliver. And Mrs Mack wondered whether her efforts up till now had been enough, whether they in any way matched Mr Graham's efforts then.

As she looked into the depths of her own soul she was distressed to find that perhaps after all she was to be found wanting.

She stood up suddenly and took a deep breath.

Very well. She would start her new crusade herself now. This very night. Out there evil was stalking the environs of Glendarroch. She would carry a torch of lightness into the dark places and bring about her own spiritual and moral revival.

The torch of light which she was about to take out with her required a practical torch to show her the way, so she reached down the heavy duty one which stood on the shelf by the back door and put it on the kitchen table. Then, placing her hat on her head as though it were a brightly plumed helmet, she jabbed it into place with an immense hatpin with a cairngorm on its end, shrugged herself into her heavy winter overcoat and on an impulse, feeling that the battle might perhaps become physical rather than spiritual, she took her umbrella as well.

She had a last look round the kitchen. It seemed cosy in the warm glow of the electric light and the heat from the Aga cooker on which the pot with the rabbit in it was simmering gently, and for a moment her new-found resolution failed her. Out there was darkness and cold, mystery and uncertainty. Here there was security and peace.

She squared her shoulders resolutely. This would not do. The devil was tempting her to give up her new-found mission and she snapped her fingers in his face. God helps those who help themselves.

Besides, there were things happening out there which everyone else seemed to know about and she didn't.

And that wouldn't do at all.

She opened the back door, shivering as the icy cold of the outdoors met her, closed it and locked it, pocketing the key.

Then, the torch playing on the garden path ahead of her, she set off with determined stride out into the unknown.

2

Archie was not happy. It was all right when he was one of a team because then he could hide amongst the crowd and not get too involved or hide himself behind a larger member. Then he was there but wasn't conspicuous in any way. But now here he was stuck out in the wild miles from anywhere all on his own waiting for he didn't know what, except that there was likely to be a sub-machine gun at the end of it.

He began to regret his chivalrous decision to come and join the hunt. It may have impressed Mrs Cunningham but it would have been much better if he had simply stayed at Glendarroch House and manned the telephone for her. After all, there were those two poor women alone in that huge place. What would happen if the gang decided to attack there instead? Suppose all this talk of raiding the deer farm was only a feint, and Joe MacMorran had actually brought in assistants to make a frontal attack on the lady laird whom he apparently hated? It was a bit ridiculous to think of himself stuck out here uselessly while Glendarroch House was being set on fire by a horde of hoodlums from Glasgow. He should have thought where his primary duty lay.

But he had gone too far now. To desert his post at this juncture would mean that there would be an enormous gap in their defences. And furthermore it would be just his luck if the gang decided to attack through the gate where he was standing at this moment, and if he wasn't there questions might be asked in the village, awkward questions which he would find it uncomfortable to answer.

Archie was certainly not happy.

Supposing they attacked here and he was on his own?

He nervously hefted the blunderbuss in his hands and glanced round. This particular gate lay at the far side of a field in which cattle grazed contentedly in the summer. Just now it was empty. Nothing moved in it in the moonlight. Slightly to his right as he stood with his back to the gate there was a thin line of trees where the field bordered a patch of waste ground. He was thankful for the moonlight, and began to count his blessings. He might have been given one of the gates which were surrounded by undergrowth. Here at least he could be sure that no one was going to creep up on him unawares.

He shivered and began to walk along the perimeter fence towards the next gate. Dougal had said they should do this whenever the opportunity offered, and Archie hoped to catch sight of Jamie Stewart who was guarding it. He hadn't seen Jamie to speak to for some months, and it would be good to get some word of the latest on the Dougal-Morag romance straight from her father's mouth.

He approached the line of trees and prepared to pass through it. Beyond he should be able to glimpse the next gate lying in a fold of the waste ground.

The trees towered over him, black against the clear sky. Their branches seemed like claws bearing down on him and he was about to hurry to avoid their pounce when a twitch of movement caught his eye and he froze to the spot, clutching the stock of the blunderbuss in a hand which suddenly started to sweat. It was just a flash of something slipping behind one of the trees, nothing more . . .

There . . . a shape growing from the side of a tree trunk . . . Growing and swelling . . . Archie swallowed and strained to see further into the shadows. How many. . . ?

Suddenly Glendarroch House seemed infinitely desirable,

the can of baked beans ambrosia, and the stewed cup of tea nectar. He would never again complain about the draughts in the flat above the stables. In fact if he were allowed to survive he promised he would do something about them tomorrow as ever was. Not only that, but he would set about a general overhaul of Glendarroch House itself, make it wind and weatherproof again, something he had been promising to do for quite a long time. If only he were allowed to survive tonight . . .

"Archie!"

He stopped babbling prayers under his breath and peered cautiously at the shadow which had just detached itself from the tree and was walking forward towards him.

"Who—who's that?" he asked fearfully.

"Put that thing away, will you? It might go off."

Ken Calder stepped out of the shadow of the trees and Archie let his breath out with relief. He seemed to have been holding it for a couple of hours.

"Ken," he said. "I thought you were one of the gang."

"I thought *you* were."

"What's happening?"

"I hoped you'd tell me."

"I don't know. I don't know anything except that they're supposed to be around somewhere."

"I know they'll be around somewhere. But where?"

"Are the police coming?"

"I don't think so. I spoke to Murray."

"Well?"

"Let's face it, Archie, maybe I'm not the right sort of person to convince the police of something like this. Do you know what he said?"

"Not till you tell me."

" 'Are you sure you're not hallucinating again, Mr Calder?' he said. I nearly socked him one, but that wouldn't have done much good. I told him I haven't touched a drop for months. Offered to take a breath test there and then, but he said that was only for motoring offences."

"You mean he's not coming?"

"I mean exactly that. Not on my say-so. I tried. But I could see I wasn't going to get anywhere, so I came away and got back here as fast as I could. What's going on?"

"Dougal's got us all spread out guarding the gates, but there aren't enough of us. There's several gates not guarded at all just now."

"I'll take one, then. Which?"

"He had to leave the ones furthest from the road unguarded. He thought the gang was less likely to get in there."

"That's true."

"And he said to take a walk along the perimeter fence every now and then, meet up with whoever's on the next gate, that sort of thing. That's what I was doing when you nearly gave me a heart attack just now."

"Fine. Who's on the next one that way?"

"One of the Moncurs, I think. But the gate beyond that's not guarded."

"Okay. I'm on my way— What's that?"

They whirled round as a twig cracked with the force and surprise of a rifle shot not fifteen yards away. Archie, encouraged by the presence of reinforcements, levelled the blunderbuss in the direction of the noise.

"All right, whoever you are, come out of there with your hands up," he called softly.

A figure emerged from almost the same place Ken had emerged from.

"You've been watching too many war films, Archie," said Brian Blair.

Archie lowered the blunderbuss again.

"I know I'm a very popular character around here," he said, "but why does everyone choose to visit me at this time of night?"

"We can't resist your conversation, Archie," said Brian. "And I suppose you could say that we feel safer when you're around, wouldn't you Ken?"

"I'd have said so, yes. Especially with that thing you've got there. It would strike fear into the Light Brigade."

"And probably did," said Brian.

"What's happening?" asked Archie.

"Nothing," said Brian. "Nothing at all. I've been right round the fence and there's no sign of bandits. You're the first people I've come across. How long have you been here?"

"Not more than half an hour," said Archie, though it felt

longer. He explained again about what Dougal had organised and Brian nodded approval.

"There's nothing much else we can do," he said.

"Except go home to our beds," suggested Archie.

"No. They'll come," said Brian. "There won't be much sleep for any of us tonight."

"You really think they'll come?" Archie enquired.

Brian nodded.

"As sure as Christmas," he said.

3

Dougal thought quickly. This altered his whole concept of what should be done to save the deer farm. Before, it had been a question of keeping the gang out, not letting them near the animals. Already that had failed. Now it called for more desperate measures, and they would have to be taken quickly and efficiently. There was very little time left to them.

"I'm going in after them," he whispered to Jimmy.

"Okay. I'll come with you."

"No, you won't."

"Dougal, you can't go after them on your own. There are four of them and one of them—"

"One of them has a sub-machine gun, I know," said Dougal tersely.

"Well, you can't tackle them single-handed."

"Better single-handed than double-handed or more. There's less chance of someone getting hurt."

"Look, Dougal—"

"Keep your voice down!"

"But—"

"Quiet, I said!"

Jimmy obediently lowered his voice to match Dougal's hoarse whisper.

"All right, but what about all the shouting you were asking for just ten minutes ago?"

"That was when they were outside. Anything to stop them from getting in. Scare them away. But now they are in that's no use any more. If they hear us they may open up on the deer in a panic. We can't have that."

"I don't see how you're going to stop them."

"I've got an idea. It's maybe not brilliant, but it's all I can think of."

He began to scrabble around in the loose stony ground at the gate in the light of the torch. He found a flat, black stone about six inches across and after hacking at it with his heel, managed to dislodge it from the frozen ground. He tested its weight in his hand and grunted in approval before he thrust it into his pocket. Again he searched and found another, similar stone, perhaps a fraction bigger.

"What do you want me to do?" asked Jimmy.

Dougal thought.

"I'd like it if you could get help at this gate, because this is the one they'll try to escape from. But there mustn't be any noise. That means you can't shout for help."

"I could go and get it. Bob's just back there—"

"No. The gate mustn't be left. They could come back at any time. You'll have to look after it yourself, Jimmy. All right?"

"Of course."

"But don't do anything silly. If they come running, make sure they're not armed. If they are, get yourself well hidden, then shout for help."

"You don't want silence then?"

"Once they're on the run, silence won't matter any longer. If they're not armed, try to stop at least one of them."

"Okay, but I don't like it, Dougal."

"Neither do I. But the deer aren't going to like what this lot are planning for them either."

He turned for the gate and Jimmy stopped him with a hand on his elbow.

"Don't do anything stupid, either, Dougal," he said.

"I won't. I'm not a hero, you know."

Jimmy grinned at him encouragingly.

"I'm not so sure of that," he said.

Dougal stared at him for a moment, then nodded and headed into the deer farm. Jimmy watched as the figure grew dim and faded from sight. Then he thrust his hands deep into his pockets and, taking up position in the shadow of a chestnut tree, he settled down to wait.

4

Joe MacMorran came down on to what was becoming for him a familiar part of the Glendarroch-Auchtarne road. The little natural lay-by formed by the gate in the fence was overhung by the branches of trees and surrounded by hedges, and in the silver moonlight he began to feel that he knew every inch of it.

He shivered from the intense cold which had developed since darkness had gathered. Overhead the sky was crystal clear, ablaze with stars, and the gibbous moon swung higher, shortening the shadows, almost as bright as day where there was nothing to shade its light. It was a breathlessly still night, no sound round him at all, no wind to stir the branches, no distant rumble of traffic such as he had been used to and comforted by all his life, nothing but the absolute stillness of a country winter night. To him it was something he had never experienced before, strange and alien, almost menacing.

Thank God for the moonlight. Had there been no moon or had it been cloudy he knew he would have been standing here in a darkness which he could almost feel, without a street light or a neon sign to break the unnatural blackness of it all.

He shivered again and this time it was not entirely from the cold. There is a dread in everyone of the unknown and the unknowable, and to Joe the silence and the silvery moonlight were things which he, coming from a city where the lights killed all natural darkness, did not understand.

As he stood there leaning against the gate, waiting, ears strained for some familiar sound, he began to pick up small noises he hadn't heard before. Small, surreptitious noises like the creak of a frost-snapped twig or the rustle of some small nocturnal creature hurrying for warmth and shelter before the cold killed it.

And there was another noise from the road in the direction of Glendarroch. It was a slight noise, unidentifiable, and had it not been for the silence he wouldn't have noticed it. He swung round towards it, feeling his heart beating a little harder, but there was nothing to see. There the road entered a tunnel of trees, and although the branches were bare and skeletal in the March night they killed the light from the moon sufficiently to make vision impossible, and he wasn't sure what it was that had attracted his attention.

But then, before he had a chance to start worrying about it, to feel the primeval panic terror seize him, a dull rumble began to grow from the direction of Auchtarne, a reassuring, man-made rumble and a little afterwards lights flickered along the hedgerows, approaching him.

A minute later the refrigerator van came to a halt beside him with a gentle squeal of brakes. He had half-expected something bigger, a huge articulated juggernaut, but he had warned Prettyboy that the track was not a three-lane motorway and Prettyboy had evidently heeded his words. This was a comparatively small four-wheel truck and in the moonlight he could make out the words *Bartlett's Beautiful Fresh Frozen Foods* painted on the side. He found himself looking up at a face which grinned down from the cab.

"Hi," said the face. "I was tellt to stoap wance and ask for Joe. You him?"

Joe grinned his relief back.

"Got it in wan, chum, got it in wan," he said. "You Eric?"

"The same in person."

"Can ye get this thing up the track here?"

"Let's have a shufty," said Eric and, leaving the engine running, he opened the cab door and climbed out.

He helped Joe open the gate and had a look up the track.

"Does it get any steeper?"

"No."

"No twists and turns, eh?"

"No. Just straight up to the turning place."

"No bother, then. Piece of cake."

"Right. Better get it off the road before anyone sees it. I'll close the gate and follow. See ye up there."

Eric got into the cab again, reversed carefully for a few feet and then swung the van into the track and bounced gently but steadily up. It was a good size of van, thought Joe. Big enough for the carcasses. Not too big for the track.

He closed the gate and rechained it, leaving it as it was and trotted up the track in the wake of the van.

He could hear the engine labouring somewhat up the slope and it was as though that noise were the signal for all other noises. Perhaps the van had awoken life which would otherwise have stayed asleep until daylight or warmer weather, but suddenly there seemed movement all round him, branches of trees still swaying wildly where the van had forced its way past them, and the sound and the movement were all comforting. It was as though civilisation had forced its way back into the forefront of his mind and he forgot that strange panic he had felt in the road just before the van had arrived.

He found the van stopped in the turning point and even as he got there he saw the lights go out and heard the engine die. With the extinguishing of the lights and the death of the engine the silence of the night drew round them again.

Eric climbed down and Joe saw a sudden flare of light as he lit a cigarette.

"Good journey?" he asked.

"No bother," said Eric. "How's things your end?"

"Fine. I seen them going into the farm. You timed it nicely. They should start bringing the carcasses down in the land-rover in a minute or two."

"Great. I dinna want to be here too long. Got to get them back to Glasgow and oot the van before daylight."

"Aye."

"Hoo many carcasses?"

"Mebbe aboot a hundred."

Eric whistled.

"That'll be a tight squeeze," he said. "If I'd kent I'd have brung the bigger van."

"Ye'd no have gotten a bigger wan up the track."

"Aye, well, that's true too."

They stood silently, listening. Joe wasn't sure whether they would hear The Progger's Sterling-Patchett from here. It was a silenced weapon, he knew, but no silenced weapon was completely silent and in this stillness sound carried a long way. He supposed it would depend on where they found the deer, but suddenly, with the enterprise so near completion, and the best part of a thousand quid just about safe in his pocket, this inaction became unbearable.

"Listen, Prettyboy wants to make a quick get-out," he said. "Ye'd better turn the van, maybe, ready to start."

"Aye, right."

Eric threw away his cigarette stub and turned for the cab.

And at that moment from higher up the hill came the sudden short sharp stutter of the Sterling-Patchett.

5

From the shelter of a clump of dead bracken, Dougal could see the men about fifty yards in front of him. They were standing upright, spread out in a long line, and they were advancing with a definite purpose. The herd must be ahead of them, beyond the ridge over which Dougal could not yet see, but from the attitude of the men he knew that they knew where they were going.

He wished he'd brought his shotgun with him after all. In spite of the threat of court action hanging over him he would dearly have liked the comfort of his gun now. It would be worth it to take a pot shot at this lot, and if he hit one or more of them, well, there was probably a limit to what the court could do to him. And this time he had proof that they were poaching, not just taking a quiet evening stroll.

But he had no gun. He had no weapon of any kind. And there were four of them. And once again he told himself that one of them had a sub-machine gun. It was a fact which he didn't need to repeat. He knew it well enough already, but the thought kept coming back into his mind, concentrating it wonderfully.

The herd, he knew, must be about a hundred yards ahead of the gang, probably moving away from them because although there was no wind they would hear the men and there would be uneasiness in them at the strange sounds which were moving in their direction. Over the months the deer had become remarkably tame, but it was principally the Argocat they recognised, associating it with the arrival of food, and without it human presence still disturbed them.

His mind was working clearly now, sharp and incisive

under the pressure of urgency.

The second man from the left was the one to watch. He could see the gun cradled in his arms.

They had a plan, a crude plan, but one which was bound to work. They were moving the deer gently away from them, but some two hundred yards ahead was the fence bounding this division of the farm, keeping the deer in the one comparatively small area so that they did not overcrop what little natural feed there was at this time. Whether the men were aware of what they were doing or not, they were actually driving the deer into a corner.

He hefted the flat disc of stone which he had picked up at the gate and then began to crawl forward towards the men, surmounting a slight rise as they disappeared down the other side, and as he looked down at the new vista which opened up before him in the pale moonlight he saw that what he feared had actually happened.

The herd was ahead, moving gently into the corner of the division, bunching closer together as their area of freedom contracted, a moving mass of hinds, and amongst them he could pick out the alert head and the magnificent antlers of Achilles. They were not panicking, just a little restless and uneasy as the men moved down the slope towards them.

Dougal had been moving with caution and in utter silence, unlike the men who were making no attempt to disguise their presence and whom he could have followed by sound alone had the night been dark. But now time was short and speed was more important than silence.

He began to gain on them, crouched almost on all fours for a quick burst across open ground, eyes peeled to spot any sign of one of the men turning his head to look behind him.

Thirty yards away, and now the men slowed their pace. They knew the deer were trapped. They had no need for hurry now or even caution.

Dougal closed the gap and dropped flat as he sensed the rightmost man turn and glance behind him. There was no cry of alarm so, raising his head slowly, and only a fraction, he saw the man had turned back, unsuspecting, and was watching the deer again.

Dougal closed the gap further, but with every lessening

of the distance silence became more important. He didn't want to be spotted. The second man from the left still had the gun cradled in his arms, but there was absolutely no cover here and if they became aware of his presence Dougal was a sitting target.

Using elbows only now he pulled himself through the cold, brittle undergrowth, cursing the fact that the frost had come to take away the wet moistness of the vegetation which helped to kill sound. Everything around him was rustling like a Christmas tree. He must surely be heard.

But the men's thoughts were on other things. He stopped again and risked another lift of the head to study the situation. They were spread out maybe fifteen yards apart, standing in a rough semicircle round the angle of the fences which contained the herd.

And Dougal was still twenty yards away. Too far.

Picturing vividly what was going to happen within the next half minute unless he could stop it, he wormed his way forward once more, conscious of the rough ground tearing at the elbows of his anorak, feeling the coating of frost melting on him and soaking through his clothing . . .

The man second on the left would uncradle the sub-machine gun. He would sight to the left of the herd. He would pull the trigger and as he did so he would swing the gun in a wide, graceful arc through forty or fifty degrees, pumping a hail of lead into the helpless animals penned in front of him . . .

And even as he drew the picture in his mind he was conscious of the man begin the action which he had envisaged. He saw the arms move and the angle of the gun in them changed.

Dougal rose to his feet, uncaring now whether they saw him or not. He drew back the arm with the stone in it as the man brought the gun to the firing position at his hip and then let it go as though he were skimming a stone into the sea from a beach.

And as he did so he knew he had aimed true. He had already drawn the second stone from his pocket when he knew it would not be needed. He leapt forward, following his primary attack.

From that distance the stone could scarcely have missed and it had all the strength of Dougal's anger behind it.

Dougal was within four yards of the man when the stone struck him in the small of the back. The impact made him throw his arms into the air and his finger must already have been on the trigger for there was the staccato tattoo of firing, not as loud as Dougal had expected, the bullets going high and harmless into the air, and then the man was falling forward and Dougal was on top of him.

He wasn't really watching the man. His eyes were on the gun. That was what mattered, and when it fell from the man's grasp he forgot about him and lunged for it, seizing it clumsily by the barrel, and wielding it like a club as the man came to his feet and staggered towards him.

The blow caught the man on the side of the temple and he went down like an ox, and Dougal had never felt such a sense of fierce satisfaction in his life.

He whirled round, brandishing the gun, ready to face whatever the other three might be contemplating, but of the other three there was no sign.

Neither was there a sign of the herd.

The chatter of fire must have finally panicked the deer and they had broken loose from the restraint of the fence angle, heading for the open ground and safety. And the only way they could do that was forward between the men. Now they were scattered. Dougal could see odd pockets of animals heading away up the hillside, seeking the sanctuary of higher ground.

He breathed heavily and looked round. The man he had felled lay limp and unmoving, and even as he made sure that he was only unconscious—for he had struck out very hard indeed in the strength of his hatred and fear and might well have crushed his temple and therefore his life—he heard a muffled cry for help some distance away across the open ground.

Carefully putting the safety catch back on the sub-machine gun he hurried in the direction of the sound and there was one of the men, crouched and holding his right leg in both hands, and Dougal could see in the silver light a black stain spreading on the trouser leg.

He was a big man, heavy and muscular but not terribly fit from the look of him. Certainly not now.

He looked up at Dougal, his face twisted in pain.

"Here," he said. "I never kent they was dangerous. I

thought they was quiet things. Wouldna say boo to a goose."

"They don't usually," said Dougal.

"If I'd of kent I'd never of come. For God's sake, will ye do something for this leg of mine?"

"I'm not sure that I should. You wouldn't have done much for the deer, would you?"

"Dangerous things. God. It came for me that fast I'd no time to get oot of the way."

Dougal knelt down beside him and looked at the torn trouser leg. There seemed to be a big puncture in the man's thigh and the blood was welling fast. He unbuckled his anorak and pulled out the belt and began to make a tourniquet.

And as he did so he grinned savagely in satisfaction.

In the panic to get away Achilles must have collided with the man and those magnificent antlers had done the work normally reserved for fighting off a rival stag in the rutting season.

Achilles had taken his own revenge.

6

Mrs Mack had first become aware of the man standing in the lay-by at the gate where the track led up to Corrie Vrannichan before he became aware of her, and she slipped quietly out of his sight just as she saw his head come up with a jerk and peer down the road in her direction. He was a shadowy figure in the shelter of the trees and yet she had no difficulty in recognising him. It was the man she had spoken to in the church, the man who had told her those appalling falsehoods about being a divinity student who had had to abandon his studies to take care of a sick family after his father had died. Had circumstances been different Mrs Mack might have gone straight up to him and assaulted him physically with her umbrella, so indignant was she at the way he had played on her inborn sympathy and natural Christian sense of care. After all, she thought, someone with the milk of human kindness in them was susceptible to any hard luck story, so it was only natural that she should have been convinced by him. But it was most annoying all the same. This was the man MacMorran. Not only had he cheated her, but he had also cheated the village and was bent on doing so again. Mrs Mack's indignation grew by leaps and bounds. For many years she had preached the fact that they were a small community fighting a hard, ruthless and thoroughly immoral world. Gradually she had seen that immorality infect Glendarroch and trying to stifle it had proved a losing battle.

Well, now was her chance to do something about it. Whatever this man was doing he was doing something illegal.

This was her opportunity to follow Mr Billy Graham.

A moment later she saw the van arrive and after a brief conversation she saw it reverse, saw MacMorran open the gate to let it drive in and then saw him close the gate after it and follow it up the track.

God helps those who help themselves, thought Mrs Mack again, and nodding to herself she plunged off the road into the undergrowth heading up towards the turning point in a more direct line than the man MacMorran. In a way she had a personal score to settle with him. An eye for an eye, as her Mr Mack used to always say.

She reached a clump of bushes overlooking the turning point just as the driver switched out the lights and turned off the engine, and she was in a grand position to hear the conversation which followed.

Her face grew more and more stern as she listened. So it was all true after all. Clearly Dougal Lachlan had been quite justified in firing at that other young man and—yes, she had to admit it—she had been wrong. She was a big enough person to admit a mistake when she had made one. After all, she was only human.

But now there was perhaps some action she could take to prevent this appalling event from taking place. She didn't fancy her chances of marching in to the deer farm and confronting the men there, especially if they were armed which, from the conversation she had overheard, they seemed to be. As far as the deer were concerned they would simply have to take their chance. But at least she could make sure that these criminal elements didn't enjoy their ill-gotten gains.

But what could she do? Confront these two now?

In spite of her moral indignation and her anxiety to help herself as God wanted her to and although she badly wanted one of MacMorran's eyes in payment for hers, she jibbed at the idea of such a confrontation, even though she had the umbrella.

She shifted uncomfortably, for the branches of the bushes she was hiding behind seemed to have wriggled round to attack her from the rear, and as she did so a branch of a tree brushed the top of her head, knocking her hat sideways. It would have been dislodged altogether if the hatpin hadn't held it in place . . .

The hatpin . . .

A sign, she thought. It really was a sign. God helps those who help themselves.

She pulled the hatpin out of the hat and looked at it.

It was indeed a very strong hatpin, a present from the late Mr Mack to commemorate their wedding anniversary the year before he died. Mr Mack had never been a believer in expensive presents, always being concerned about the sins of the flesh and declaring that one got one's reward in heaven. He was much more inclined to give practical gifts. This was one of them. And how wise he had been. The steel blade glinted in the moonlight and the cairngorm reflected it.

The two men were standing at the driver's cab, still chatting, and the far side of the cab was close to the spot where she stood hidden. She could approach the van without the slightest danger of being seen, and resolutely she stepped out of the bushes and crouched down beside the front wheel.

Wielding the hatpin like a dagger she plunged it into the wall of the tyre. The rubber was surprisingly resistant and she had to exert quite a lot of pressure to force the hatpin home, but the hatpin itself was very sharp indeed, a fact which she knew to her cost when she had sometimes affixed her hat in a hurry or a temper, causing inaccuracy of aim, and eventually she managed to drive it home to a depth of a couple of inches or so. Then she levered it around a bit, drawing it out again as she did so.

The result was disappointing. There was no sudden hiss

of escaping air which, she thought, might be just as well as it would certainly have alerted the two men still talking not six feet away from her on the other side of the van.

She tried again at a different point of the tyre wall. Again she pressed the hatpin home and levered it around before withdrawing it. The result was the same: unsatisfactory.

She tried it twice more before she became aware of movement at the far side of the van and, hastily withdrawing the hatpin from the tyre for the last time, she slipped back into the bushes and safety, clutching her loose hat firmly to her head.

She had just reached the shelter when she heard the short, sharp chatter of a gun from further up the hillside.

7

Jimmy heard the chatter of the gun and his heart sank, only to rise again almost immediately. The burst of fire had been so short that surely not many of the animals could have been killed, he thought.

Had Dougal managed to do something to prevent further destruction? He strained his ears and heard nothing. After that sudden burst of noise there was an ominous silence.

Jimmy became a prey to frightening thoughts. It had been a short burst of firing, but not too short to have been stopped by Dougal. Was that what had happened? Had Dougal been shot and was he now lying somewhere in the deer farm, perhaps badly wounded, perhaps even dead?

Jimmy bit his lip. Dougal had ordered him to stay here at the gate and not to let anyone escape. Could he continue to obey those orders now, or should he go into the farm and see if he could find Dougal? Or should he run round the perimeter fence to the next gate and seek Bob's advice? What were the others doing? Standing as he was, indecisive, unsure?

The thud of footsteps approaching the gate came as an immense relief. He had been right not to move. There was more than one set of footsteps, so it wasn't Dougal, and again he wondered what had happened to him.

But now he knew what he had to do, and he waited under the trees until he saw two figures come running for the gate and with relief he saw that neither of them carried a gun.

He stepped forward just as they reached the gate itself.

"All right," he shouted. "That's as far as you go—"

But they didn't stop. They spread out beyond the gate, heading in different directions. Jimmy launched himself at the nearer of the two. They collided with a breathtaking thump and rolled over together.

"Jimmy!"

He recognised the voice and recovered sufficient breath to shout.

"Okay, Dad! Get the other one!"

From the corner of his eye he saw his father appear from the undergrowth at the edge of the fence, but the man he had collided with was struggling to his feet and Jimmy launched himself at him again.

It was a scrappy, messy fight, unscientific and expending a great deal of energy to not much purpose, but Jimmy was the younger and the fitter and the more agile and before long the man was kneeling on the ground with his hands up in an attitude of surrender.

"All right, all right," he said, breathing heavily. "I'll go quiet. Just leave me alone, will ye?"

Jimmy nursed a bruised knuckle as he stood over him.

"Okay, who are you?" he demanded.

The man shrugged.

"Me, I'm just the driver," he said. "Dinna ken anything aboot what's going on. Just told to drive here and drive back again after. That's all. Honest."

"Oh, aye," said Jimmy. "Tell that to a soldier on a boat. We'll see what the police have to say when they get here."

"Och, no the polis. There's no need to bring them into it. Just a wee ploy, son."

"A wee ploy? Some wee ploy. Come on. I'm taking you down to the village."

The man staggered to his feet and Jimmy, looking round, listened. There seemed to be no sound anywhere now, the night had returned to its silent mystery. And then some distance away came the sudden harsh sound of a car engine starting. The man looked up quickly as the sound started and then faded, and then his shoulders sagged as though with the fading sound hope faded too.

"Seems like you're on your own," said Jimmy.

"Aye. Well, maybe," said the man. "Come on, son. Which way do we go?"

Jimmy pointed him in the right direction and followed him through the undergrowth towards the track which led to Glendarroch.

8

Brian saw the man disappear into the trees on the opposite side to that from which he had emerged. For a moment he hesitated. But Jimmy had said that he could manage the one he was contending with so he set off after the other.

But his hesitation had cost him a good deal of distance and he found that he wasn't in such good condition as he had imagined himself to be. The man had got quite far ahead and was no longer visible. But Brian could follow the sound of his progress. It wasn't difficult. The man was making as much noise as a herd of stampeding elephants.

Five minutes later he emerged from the trees on to the track. He was breathing heavily and a branch of a tree had gashed his forehead. He could feel blood oozing down his cheek but there was no pain yet.

And there, down the track, just moving out of sight round the next bend, was his quarry.

Brian set off in pursuit, moving carefully for the track was becoming very treacherous as the frost hardened, freezing the puddles which had been caused by the earlier rain.

The track twisted and turned tortuously and the figure in front of him was more often out of sight than in, but suddenly he came to a long straight stretch and he stopped, puzzled. There was no sign of anyone on the track ahead, and he was sure that the man couldn't have got as far as the next bend.

That meant he must have turned off and was probably hiding, so Brian drew to a halt, panting. He didn't want to face an ambush. The man could be concealed anywhere just off the track in the depths of the trees and bushes and jump him as he went past.

And then suddenly there was the stutter of an engine about a hundred yards ahead, and Brian cursed. He should have thought. Of course they would have a vehicle fairly close for the carcasses. He set off again, but his foot slipped in a frozen puddle and he went all his length, jarring his elbow as he did so.

As he struggled to his feet he saw the land-rover burst out of the bushes at the edge of the track, swing hard to the right and start bouncing its way downwards towards the turning point.

Brian stood up slowly and watched it go. There was nothing more he could do. He dusted himself down and nursed the throbbing in his elbow. Not much damage done, he thought, but he reckoned from what had been going on on the hillside that night that there would be a lengthy queue at Dr Wallace's surgery in the morning.

9

The sound of the gun fire galvanised Joe and Eric into activity.

"That's it," said Joe. "They've got them. They'll start bringing them down any minute. Hurry!"

Eric got into the cab and the engine roared into life. There was a clash of gears and then the van lumbered backwards a few yards, turning in towards the gate to the track which led upwards towards the deer farm.

Suddenly there was a lurch and Eric stopped and turned off the engine.

Joe hurried forward as he got out and came round to the other side of the cab.

"What's up?" he asked.

"Aye. I thought it. Steering suddenly went all heavy. See there. A flat."

Joe stared at the nearside front wheel aghast. It was only too true, the bottom rim of the wheel rested on the ground, the tyre spread out loosely around it.

He swore quietly and fluently for quite a long time and then pulled himself together.

"We'll need to change it," he said. "How long'll it take?"

Eric shrugged.

"There's a spare all right, but they're hell to get off," he said. "Lend a hand."

Joe nodded and fidgetted while Eric got out the jack and began slowly and laboriously to raise the side of the van. Joe got out the spare wheel and trundled it forward ready to replace, and all the time his ears were listening for the sound of the land-rover making its first journey down from the farm with the first of the carcasses. So far there was nothing, and in a way that was a relief. He didn't want to be caught by Prettyboy in this predicament. Not that the flat tyre was his fault. It was just an unfortunate accident and with any luck it shouldn't delay the getaway for more than ten minutes or so.

Eric was leaning on the fulcrum of the spanner, muttering and sweating in spite of the cold as he tried to loosen the first of the wheel nuts. Joe went to help and they leant their combined weight on the long bar. At last it shifted, stopped, shifted again and then moved freely.

"Wonder what caused that?" Eric muttered as he adjusted the spanner on the next nut. "These damned tracks are full of sharp stones, I suppose."

Further conversation was abandoned as they put their weight on the fulcrum again.

As they managed to loosen the last and most stubborn of the nuts Joe heard what he had been waiting for, the sound of the land-rover engine.

"Here they come," he shouted, and left Eric and hurried to the gate to open it and let the land-rover through.

Eric removed the last of the nuts and manhandled the wheel off the hub, laying it on the ground beside the spare.

Lights flickered over the van as the land-rover approached.

It seemed to be coming at a fair lick and Joe wondered what had caused this urgency.

Scruffy had better start braking soon, he thought, or there would be trouble, but then he suddenly realised that Scruffy wouldn't know that the van was blocking the gate, and he began to hurry up the track to wave him down as soon as he appeared round the last bend.

The lights straightened and Joe waved with increasing

urgency, but the land-rover didn't seem to be stopping. He waved more frantically, but it didn't make any difference. At the last moment when the blazing headlights were almost on top of him he leapt aside into a tangle of bushes as the land-rover hurtled past him and it was only after that that he saw the sudden red flare of light as the driver became aware of what lay ahead and stamped hard on the brakes.

The land-rover lurched and bounced and the wheels locked on one of the frozen puddles. It shot through the gate and struck the rear of the van. The van jerked forwards off the jack so that it seemed to be standing for a moment on only three wheels. Then it teetered and collapsed sideways as though it had suddenly fallen asleep and the land-rover, its front stove in, its windscreen shattered, subsided with a sigh as though it were glad its life were finally over and it could rest in peace at last.

Joe stared aghast at the wreckage and then began to run forward to the land-rover just as Eric came round the side of the drunken van.

"Bloody hell," he said. "What is this? Stock car racing? If I'd kent it'd be like this I'd never have came—"

"Shut up and lend a hand," snapped Joe as he tried to force open the driver's door of the land-rover. It was jammed and it took some force to prise it open. Eventually it shifted with a screech of protesting metal.

It wasn't Scruffy driving. It was Prettyboy. He didn't look very pretty now. He was slumped over the steering wheel, blood welling from a cut in his forehead, unconscious.

That, thought Joe irrelevantly, is what comes of not wearing your seat belt.

And at that moment two things happened simultaneously. Men began to appear running down the track towards them, and when Joe turned with an instinctive idea of getting down the further track to the road and possible escape he saw headlights coming towards him up the track. A white car appeared and on the top of it was the blue flashing light of the police.

Joe looked at Eric and Eric looked at Joe in silence. And then at precisely the same moment they both gave vent to precisely the same four letter word.

10

"Dougal wreaked havoc," said George Carradine appreciatively. "A great deal of havoc. And it would seem he's got
away with it. Gun shot wounds in the leg, one man with a
broken rib, not to speak of another one gored by a frantic
stag, though I don't suppose one can lay that at Dougal's
door. That's not a bad score, Elizabeth."

Elizabeth smiled.

"And not an animal lost," she said.

She held up the brandy bottle but he shook his head.

"I have to drive home, remember," he said, "and the
roads round here don't seem terribly safe these days."

"It's all ended remarkably well," said Elizabeth. "I
suppose Dougal will be all right now, will he?"

"Perfectly all right. I had a word with Paterson before I
came over. Murdoch's evidence was just what was needed,
and it led the police to find further evidence near the same
spot. Fuses and wire and so on. There's no doubt at all
that the men were poaching. The fiscal will drop the
assault with a deadly weapon charge in view of the
changed circumstances."

"What about the young one—the one who got shot?"

"I think he'll be all right. After all, he wasn't concerned
in the attack on the deer farm. And he did give warning of
it. That'll be taken into account. He'll probably be let off
with a fairly stiff caution and a warning that next time he
won't be so lucky."

"If there is a next time. Perhaps he's learnt his lesson."

"Perhaps he has. Stranger things have happened, I
suppose." He carefully dropped an inch and a half of cigar
ash into the ash tray at the side of his chair. "The others
are being charged with rustling, you know. That's a very
much more serious crime than poaching. It could involve
heavy sentences, especially in view of their past records."

"Good," said Elizabeth. She had absolutely no sympathy
with such people. "I worry, though, George," she went on
after a few minutes of companionable silence. "We are
terribly vulnerable. It could so easily happen again. And
next time we might not be so lucky."

"I know. You will have to take as many precautions as
you can. You will need to have the fence round the farm

electrified to give warning if it's tampered with in any way."

"That will cost money."

"It'll probably cost you less in insurance if you do it. And it'll certainly be cheaper than losing your entire stock."

"Very true." She looked thoughtfully into the fire for a few moments. "You know, George, I take some comfort from this little episode," she said at last.

"I'm glad to hear there is some to take."

"Yes, there is. Do you realise how the whole community pulled together on this? Every single person in Glendarroch. In a way it justifies what I have always believed. That we are a little community here, self-sufficient, sharing everything. Murdoch is a disreputable old poacher, we all know that, even though he is the clerk to the kirk session. Yet he provided the evidence to prove that Dougal was right, in spite of the fact that he and Dougal haven't exactly seen eye to eye for some time. And the way everyone banded together to save the deer. Even Mrs Mack."

"A highly unlikely desperado."

"I know. She even confessed to feeling disappointed when she thought she'd failed to puncture that tyre."

"It must have been the pressure of the wheel turning that finally forced it to collapse."

"The tyre must have been like a colander by then."

"Indeed."

"Who would have thought of her touring the neighbourhood puncturing tyres with a hatpin to prevent the ungodly from getting away? Oh, we have our little differences but we are just like any family. Arguing, squabbling, but when the chips are down, banding together to hold the things we believe important together."

George nodded slowly and perhaps a little wistfully.

"With you as the *materfamilias*, I presume."

"Not from choice. From chance, if you like. But yes, that's what I am, I suppose."

She stretched her legs towards the fire and took a sip of brandy.

"And I must say on an occasion like this it makes me

rather proud and humble to be so," she said.

11

The blockhouses had gone. They had used explosives to destroy the underground complex and now it had disappeared. That morning she had watched the last of the lorries driving slowly along the track from Laird's Point to the road and disappear towards Auchtarne. There had been new people, she knew, brought in to finish the job, but they had only been there for a day or so. Joe MacMorran was in prison. Stevie was gone.

Now the gate into what had been the Ministry of Defence complex stood open, propped there by a stone, no longer forbidding, no longer an alien corner of the land.

Fiona wandered round the area aimlessly, without purpose. Spring had come quite suddenly and the land was beginning to waken from its winter sleep. There were lambs in the fields and their plaintive call was an endless background to life. The flowers were beginning to peep nervously from the hedgerows. Soon the scars which the contractors had left at Laird's Point would be healed and the green growth would return to swallow what was left of the works of man. Until such time as the Ministry of Defence decided they wanted to build some new plaything here. If they ever did. It was more likely that they would forget about it, that it would become simply a name in a dusty file deep in some government filing cabinet.

And Stevie? Where was he?

Back in Glasgow now, she supposed, and she found herself filled with a bitter-sweet regret.

There was no love for him as there had been for Alex Geddes. But there was a tenderness and a deep affection and also gratitude for what he had done for her. Now, perhaps, she could start to live again. Now her faith in human nature had been restored to some extent. And it was Stevie who had done it.

There hadn't even been a relationship, really. They had known each other less than a week. But it had been enough to tide her over the winter.

Fiona turned and left Laird's Point and began to make her way back towards Glendarroch House.

Behind her a lark suddenly rose from the Ministry of Defence site and hovered in the air above, pouring out a trilling radiance of song in welcome to the spring.